Do   & Deceit

P.B. Alden

Buttery
Branigan
Books

Book Cover by Patricia Branigan
Illustrations by Patricia Branigan
1 edition 2023
ISBN 978-1-7361636-6-5
Library of Congress Control Number: 2022918163

For Bulk Orders visit butterybraniganbooks.com
Email: butterybraniganbooks@gmail.com

Hidden thoughts bubble to the surface
Hush dear ones
I will remedy your misfortune
For peace is only possible if everyone abides

–Anonymous

1

Walter

My perfect day starts with fresh donuts and ends with murder. Solving a brutal crime is my destiny. As I wind my way to the top of the mountain, I lick the remnants of my jelly-filled donut off my fingers. Serenity Cliff State Park has everything a criminal desires. The picturesque cliffs are beautiful and provide the optimal spot to toss a lifeless body off the edge, never to be seen again.

Lush pines line the narrow path up the mountain, making it impossible to see around the sharp curves. Hug your side of the road, and you'll scratch your door on thick pine branches. Drive in the middle, and you risk a head-on collision. I usually pick my position based on the age of my vehicle. Today I risk the scratches. Like so many things in my life, my car is starting to feel a bit old.

My forehead beads with sweat as soon as I step out of the car. Wiping my hand across my brow, I straighten my spine. No one is around, but that doesn't mean I should slack. They say, "If you don't use it, you lose it." And by golly, they are right. Nothing says you're important more than your height, and I can't afford to lose even a half-inch of my six-foot frame to slouching, no-siree bob.

Today will be a scorcher making this hike miserable for anyone who isn't working on a missing person's case. I don't mind the heat, especially when it keeps nature-loving hikers off the trails destroying evidence.

Unfortunately, it wasn't in the cards for me to be on the police force. However, no one would be the wiser because I consistently support our local law enforcement. I monitor my trusty police scanner like it's my full-time job. Major car accident? You can find me in my bright yellow safety vest with my sizable black flashlight in hand, directing traffic as if I had been an officer my whole life. Missing child? I am there handing out fliers and coordinating the search and rescue.

Several years ago, a young woman went into labor on the freeway. My quick response and knowledge of this city allowed me to beat the ambulance by five minutes. When I showed up and got in position to catch her baby, the relief on her face was payment enough for all my diligent monitoring and quick thinking. I never heard if they named the little guy after me, but I wouldn't be surprised if they did.

The title of local hero follows me wherever I go. I could go on about keeping my community safe, but I won't because the only thing that matters to me right now is finding this missing teacher. Her disappearance made the front page of the local paper. In the grainy photo, she's holding a baby and crouching near a toddler. You can tell she's a kind person and a devoted mom. A quote from her best friend reveals she would never leave her children. I can tell by how she holds them in the picture that her friend is right. Below the image are quotes from her students, each more complimentary than the last. This woman is a fundamental pillar of our community.

The police suspect her husband of foul play. Next to her photo is a mug shot of him from a DUI charge five years ago. If I were still a betting man, I would wager my house he is responsible. Her last known whereabouts were over fifty miles away in Forest City, but I wouldn't put it past the scumbag to drive a distance to hide her body in a more remote location. I need to find her body so her kids receive the justice they deserve and she can rest in peace.

Martha would be worried if she knew the park was empty. She worries enough for both of us. She is my rock, the bread to my butter. My sweetheart made sure I had all the supplies I needed—enough water for two days and snacks for at least one. After more than forty years of marriage, she still cares about me enough to ensure I'm set for a day of solving crimes. She stood at the front door in her pajamas, waving as I left. Her smile still makes my heart flutter.

The best place to begin my search is at the park's entrance. Anything can be a clue. Something as small as a hair tie, a scrap of fabric, or drag marks could help me solve this case. The North Carolina humidity always makes the arthritis in my hips worse. I reckon my bad hips are helpful in my line of work. What is the saying? Slow and steady solves the crime.

The main path follows the cliff's edge. The low wooden fence helps prevent idiots from getting too close and accidentally plummeting to their deaths. When Martha and I used to hike together in our younger days, she never got too close to the edge because she's deathly afraid of heights.

Heights don't bother me, so I carefully climb over the fence and inch my way to the ledge, peering down to the depths below. Not a darn thing is out of place. The rocks are not disturbed, and no flowers or grass has been crushed by a body tumbling down the mountain. I climb back over the fence and use my super sniffer to detect any hint of decaying flesh. The only scent that greets my nose is sweet honeysuckle and pine. The body isn't here.

I stop at the wooden arbor, constructed by a local boy scout troop years ago, marking the entrance into a forest of ancient pines. My ears perk up at the sound of swarming flies. Three vultures circle overhead.

This is it. The moment I've been searching for all my life.

Ducking under the arbor, I'm instantly relieved from the heat. The sun filters through the canopy above as I slowly make my way down the wooded trail, soft from the years of fallen pine needles. At the side of the path, I find my victim.

Damn it—a dead squirrel.

Upon closer inspection, it looks like the little fella was in mid-scream when the good Lord took him. Leaving him for an innocent animal-loving youngster to find is out of the question. I pull my evidence-collecting gloves out of my cargo short's side pocket, slip them on, and grab the carcass by its still-fluffy tail. Luckily for me, most of the body is attached. What remains are gooey chunks of rotting flesh stuck to the ground where maggots emerge from their feast.

Holding the poor little guy away from my body, I make my way back to the cliff edge and toss him over. Moments later, there is a small thud when he hits bottom.

I continue down the trail. When I'm confident this is not the site of the missing teacher's remains, I call it a day. Even though I didn't find her today, I made this path more enjoyable for the people I promised to serve and protect.

2

Journal

What a dumb gift from my good-for-nothing therapist. Whoop-de-doo, a leather-bound journal with the words "Strong and Courageous" stamped on the front cover. What a joke. My therapist was anything but strong and courageous. She abandoned me after saying she needed to take a leave of absence. She didn't look sick. Maybe she's the one with the mental illness she's always telling me about.

Come to think of it, she probably gave me this journal to remind me I'm strong and courageous. She told me to pretend I was talking to her and express all my feelings through writing. You want me to express my feelings? Well, here you go.

Let's start with that horrible cat, Peaches. I've been feeling like someone ought to kill that miserable beast, and I just might be that person. Alright, alright, relax. I didn't kill Peaches. But I'll tell you what, my sweet Sprinkles deserved a day of peace. With Peaches creeping around all hours of the day and night, my poor baby was wound tighter than an old clock.

Peaches never gives up until he finds my baby napping peacefully. That's when he starts in with the endless meowing and hissing. Strutting around proud as a peacock rubbing his dirty orange fur against the window screen, making Sprinkles throw a hissy fit. Without fail, Sprinkles takes off like a bat out of hell, knocking over anything in her way. Just the other day, she broke the blessed angel sculpture my mother gave me at my first communion. Of course, I didn't blame Sprinkles. My sweet baby can't be held responsible for what happens when a wild animal torments her.

I posted on the neighborhood Facebook page to ask the owner of the roaming cat to at least try and keep him in their yard. All I got in return were nasty jokes about how I'm a crazy cat lover. Someone had the nerve to post a meme of an idiot nursing a cat, and twenty yahoos liked it. Acting like they don't treat their fur babies like family members too. Hypocrites, I tell you. Most of them claimed Peaches saved us from the chipmunk invasion last year. My precious baby being tortured was a joke to all of them.

Can you believe they posted fliers on every pole in town for that missing cat and with a reward to boot? If you ask me, fifty dollars is a waste of money for that thing's return.

Peaches was easy to catch. He's dumber than a box of rocks. Walked right into the live trap I baited with the can of nasty tuna in oil I found at the back of the pantry. I'm glad it went to good use, even if it did stink to high heaven. No way would I eat that garbage, but that dumb cat couldn't get enough of it. I loved seeing the surprise in his eyes when he realized he was caught.

Don't get your panties in a knot for crying out loud. I put the trap at the edge of the woods, where he'd be found in a day or two. And trust me when I say it wasn't easy getting there. I had to walk through the back alley to avoid all those fancy doorbell cameras everyone has nowadays.

After the monster clawed my arm, I almost tossed the trap into the pond, Peaches and all. Bit my tongue to keep from yelping. I took a couple of deep breaths to remember my goal. I needed to teach that vile cat and his irresponsible owner a lesson. Not drown a neighborhood pet. What if one of the kids found him? I wouldn't be able to forgive myself.

You know something? My lying therapist was right. I feel downright peaceful writing about how I took care of the Peaches problem, and my fur baby is calmer too.

3

Walter

Every evening I head out on my nightly security walk as long as the weather cooperates. Our little town is usually peaceful and quiet. However, a delinquent shows up now and then, usually in the form of a young whippersnapper who thinks the world owes them something. That's why I patrol, to do my part to keep everyone safe.

Our neighborhood has one main entrance and a park in the middle for the youngsters to play safely. Most of the houses are ranch or bungalows built in the 1950s. A few homes had significant renovations when the previous owner passed away or moved to an assisted living facility, and a new family moved in. I prefer to keep our house in its original state, a sweet little bungalow with a sizable front porch. When the boys were young, sometimes it felt like the walls were closing in on us. Now that it's just Martha and me, we have more than enough room.

On the east end of our neighborhood is a protected forest. The area is one of my favorite places, with the beautiful old oaks and red maples lining a paved walking path. There's even a small pond where a couple of the neighborhood dad's like to teach their kids the fine art of fishing. Walk a half-mile in the opposite direction, and you'll be smack dab in the middle of Main Street. Once there, you can visit the local grocery store, a diner, doodad shops, or our senior center. The senior center offers plenty of activities for older people who enjoy sitting around waiting to die. They certainly do not provide activities for mature, active people like me. As a vital member of my neighborhood, I'm not interested in cards or puzzles. However, most mornings, they do offer an array of donuts for all seniors to enjoy, so I stop in as often as possible to make my twenty-dollar yearly dues worthwhile.

Tonight, the fliers for a missing cat caught my attention. They are on every pole and a couple of trees. The reward for a safe return is fifty dollars. I grab one off a light post and ponder taking all of them but decide it won't matter if other people are searching. As a retired head security officer at the local outlet mall, I honed my skills better than the average citizen and most of the officers on the force. Don't even think about stealing or painting lewd pictures in the bathroom on my watch. People were free to enjoy themselves, all thanks to me. Plus, because I'm a so-called "average" citizen, my crime-solving will be considered more impressive when I solve a significant crime.

A missing cat most likely wouldn't be classified as a significant crime. However, the cat in the picture, Peaches, has been part of this neighborhood for at least ten years. He played an important role in containing the chipmunk invasion last year. He caught three or four a night, leaving them on everyone's doorsteps, proud of his contribution to our community. I can't let that sweet boy down. He's probably trapped somewhere. Possibly in a hole, or perhaps a stray dog chased him up a tree.

I would start my search now if it weren't getting dark. On my way home, I cut through the kiddie park to confirm Peaches isn't trapped in any play equipment. I head home after I'm confident the neighborhood is secure.

4

Walter

Frank Sinatra wakes me from a sound sleep. His velvety voice drifts up the stairs from the kitchen. Martha is probably chopping veggies for the egg white scramble she makes every morning.

"Care for some healthy morning nourishment?" she yells over the music when I walk into the kitchen.

"Why can't you just say breakfast?" I mumble under my breath.

"Oh darn it, I cut my finger. Can you grab me a bandage from the bathroom, dear?" she asks sweetly.

Life with Martha is a give-and-take. She's a fantastic cook but also a klutz. Two of her fingers are wrapped in bandages from last week. Several more stick to her arm and her leg right below her knee from who knows when. So easy to lose count.

"Breakfast with a side of blood, I see," I chuckle at my joke.

She laughs her tiny laugh. I'm a lucky man to be in a wonderful marriage. She gave me two beautiful boys who have grown into men and are in no hurry to provide us with grandchildren. So my sweet Martha plays grandma to the whole neighborhood. If someone is sick or has a baby, she's the first to bring a crockpot of mac and cheese and a plate of her homemade oatmeal raisin cookies. Every Christmas, we dress up as Santa and Mrs. Claus, giving each child a present and each parent a jar of our special Christmas cheer. "Something to help you through the holidays," I joke. Martha laughs every single time. I can't imagine spending my golden years with anyone else.

"What's on your agenda for this beautiful day?" she asks, pouring me a cup of coffee.

"I think I'll try to track down Peaches. He's gone missing."

"Oh my, you best get out there and find him. There's no time for breakfast to finish cooking," Martha tells me, handing me a banana and a granola bar. "You're the hero our neighborhood needs. Peaches' owners will be happy when he's home safe. I hope it doesn't take you too long. I might be lonely in this big house all by myself." Martha smiles at me and glances around the room. She's probably trying to come up with something to do to pass the time while I'm gone.

"Let me get you some water so you won't get dehydrated," she says, filling my backpack with enough water bottles to last a week.

I hoist the pack onto my shoulder and give her a peck on the cheek. I hope she doesn't miss me too much.

5

Martha

The door closes, and the entire atmosphere of the room changes. The sun streams through the windows, the walls seem brighter, and the air smells sweeter. My jaw relaxes, and a huge grin spreads across my face.

Don't get me wrong. I love my husband. I do. However, the only time I've been alone in the last two months is during Walter's evening strolls around the neighborhood or when he is working "a case." I was a bit disappointed when the lost teacher turned up so quickly. It turns out she was in Vegas with her teenage lover by her side. The student-turned-lover boy toy used her credit card to order room service, and there went my me time.

My life is on a permanent spin cycle, the same day after day, with no end in sight. Wake up, eat breakfast, do mundane chores, eat lunch, go to the store or the library, eat dinner, watch boring TV, and go to bed. I am a happy person. I could be content with anyone, doing almost anything. But at times, the boredom of it all gets to me. There are days I want to be lonely. I want to experience the yearning for a companion. The last time I felt that was when Walter's mom died, and he had to spend two weeks clearing her house. That was over a decade ago. What an amazing two weeks.

The year Walter retired, we did our own thing. I went to the store, and then he would go. We might as well have been flushing money down the toilet, throwing out moldy fruit and veggies because we both bought the same things. I tried making a list and sending him, but I missed walking down every aisle to see what struck my fancy for the week's meals. So I took over the weekly shopping. Without fail, Walter would call me several times, interrupting my thoughts, to tell me he had forgotten to write something on the list. The list that's magnetized to the fridge with a pen attached. We both concluded that it made the most sense to go together.

A year after he retired, we decided to downsize to one car. What's the point of paying car insurance for two cars when one only sits in the driveway? Having one car was an easy way to save money. Our old Buick is reliable, but I do miss zipping around in my little Volkswagen Bug.

I have learned that compromise is the backbone of a healthy marriage. I read once that you should view your marriage like your stocks. You wouldn't sell a stock that had performed well for years if it had an off-quarter. You would hold on to it because it will come back around. I often think of that when Walter is pestering me. I can't even enjoy *Jeopardy* with him trying to answer all the questions or laughing at his own jokes. But even on our off days, he holds his value, and he is the man I fell in love with so long ago.

I'm not going to lie, though. Spending a couple of hours alone in the house is like a vacation at a fancy spa. What should I do first? Read my book in peace. Take a bath without being asked how much longer. Watch whatever I want on TV. Or I can make myself a snack. Yes, something decadent, all to myself without thinking about making sure Walter eats something healthy. His cholesterol was through the roof at his last check-up. He must have bad genes. My cholesterol is picture-perfect, and we eat the same food.

I am as fit as a fiddle and always have been. It caused a bit of jealousy when I was younger. My co-workers wished they were like me. The other office staff and dental assistants constantly talked about the fad diets and the latest fitness craze while I ate my sandwich, chips, and cookies having nothing to add to their conversation. They power-walked around the block while I lounged in the break room alone, reading the latest best seller. Maybe I should have pretended I struggled with my weight to make at least a few friends. Back then, I wasn't good at lying. With age, you learn that there are varying degrees of truth. I have honed my skills to keep the peace with Walter.

I throw the egg white scramble in the sink and watch the garbage disposal eliminate any evidence of the "good for you" breakfast. What I wouldn't do for a donut right now, but I swore those off years ago in my quest to keep Walter healthy. I grab my chocolate chips from the veggie drawer in the refrigerator and throw in a handful of peanuts. As the chocolate melts in the microwave, my stomach growls in anticipation. Finally—a snack all to myself.

Plopping down on the sofa, I put my feet on the coffee table and turn on an old episode of *Dateline*. The show's byline, "DON'T WATCH ALONE," flashes on the screen.

"I think I'll risk it this time." I laugh at my joke.

6

Walter

As I round the corner to the neighborhood park, I spot the world's most annoying retired police officer, Frank. His self-confidence is unwarranted. He's so full of himself. How does his cap fit on his gigantic inflated head? Frank sits on a bench studying his phone like he's trying to disarm a bomb. I pivot, hurrying in the opposite direction, but not before he spots me. The old fart might be as deaf as a stone, but his eyesight is fantastic.

"Hey, Wally, fancy meeting you here," he calls out loudly, startling several birds from a nearby tree.

Mind you, there is only one thing I dislike more than seeing Frank while I am trying to solve a crime, and that is when he calls me Wally. Even though I'm two inches taller than him, he still manages to look down on me and call me the silly name only the woman who gave birth to me was allowed to use.

"What's your plan for this gorgeous day?" he yells as I meander over.

"I'm out for a walk enjoying the beautiful weather. What are you up to?" I ask, hoping he somehow didn't notice the fliers.

"I'm pretty sure we are doing the same thing," he smirks, pulling one of the missing cat fliers out of his pocket. "How about we sweeten the deal? Care to wager a little money?" he asks, reaching for his wallet. "How about a Jackson? Unless you're not up to taking on an actual police officer."

"Retired police officer," I remind him. "I'm sure I've solved as many crimes as you have. If I recall correctly, you were a meter maid those last couple of years, weren't you?"

"After being shot in the line of duty, I worked for the city in various positions. Did any of those kids with spray paint ever shoot you, Wally?"

I am not a violent person. However, at that moment, nothing would have given me more pleasure than to knock that smug expression off his stupid face.

"Nope, I was too busy busting thieves and taking names. I'm up for the challenge. You're on. I'll stop by your house after I return Peaches, and you can pay me your twenty. It's going to be a great day for WALTER." I emphasize my proper name, walking away as quickly as possible, glancing up at every tree.

"Don't bother with the trees. I have already inspected them. Like always, you're ten steps behind. Hope you have my money because I would hate to ask your sweet Martha for it and ruin her opinion of you." Somehow he always gets the last word.

I decide to walk towards town. The little diner that serves the greasy fries Martha hates would be a good place to start my search.

"Here, kitty kitty," I call out.

A mangy tabby peers up from his breakfast of a large rat carcass or some chicken bones. No way would Peaches hang around with this yellow-eyed stray stalking about.

I make my way to the senior center to scour the parking lot and search under all the shade trees and around the trash cans. Peaches is nowhere in sight. As long as I'm here, I might as well grab a couple of donuts to keep my energy up for the hunt. Two donuts left, so I take one for each hand. This is going to be my lucky day.

I walk down the alley behind the grocery store, trying to make my footsteps light. Calling might be the wrong way to capture Peaches. Sneaking up on him is a better idea. I check behind the recycling bins. Nothing. Not even a stray. Our little grocery store takes pride in being the cleanest in the state, inside and out.

The automatic doors slide open, and the cool air is a welcome relief. I spot my favorite cashier, Fran. She usually works behind the customer service counter where they keep the lotto tickets. For a moment, I envision spending all of my soon to be reward money on scratch-offs. But Martha doesn't like to spend money on wasteful things; unfortunately, she considers the lotto wasteful. The last time I played was on Christmas when she stuffed a few dollar scratchers in my stocking. Maybe I could splurge and buy a few tickets with the twenty I get from Frank when I find Peaches. Martha would never know.

"Good morning, hon. Are you feeling lucky today?" Fran asks in her sweet southern drawl.

Seeing her smile makes me feel lucky. I would never say that aloud, mind you. I'm crazy about Martha, but there's something about how Fran wears her wispy brunette hair up in that bun and lights up when I walk up to her counter. She reminds me of a girl named Susan I dated back in high school. Sweet to the core, and we were so in love. Such is life when you are young; things don't always work out as you hope.

"I am feeling lucky," I tell her. "But before I can buy any of your winners, I need to find the lost neighborhood cat." I hold up my phone to show her a picture of Peaches sitting like royalty on my porch swing.

"What a cute kitty. Sorry, the only cat I saw today was lounging on my bed when I left for work this morning."

"Thank you for your help anyway." I slide my phone back into my pocket.

I ask each cashier and two stockers. None have seen a stray cat, but two of them tell me they saw the fliers and ask me to share the reward money if I'm the one to find Peaches.

"WHEN I find Peaches," I correct them and add, "I don't think so."

I wave goodbye to Fran and my soon-to-be scratch-offs as I head out the door.

7

Martha

The credits on *Dateline* roll across the screen, and a nap sounds delightful. So you know what? That's what I'll do. In the spare bed with the brand-new pillows and fancy sheets I use just for company. Guess who's the company today.

8

Walter

The search is not going as well as I expected. I head back to the wooded area, praying Peaches didn't get in a fight with a possum and end up dead. Frank is walking down the trail next to the woods, peering up into the trees. He hasn't found Peaches. With a spring in my step, I stroll over to a row of giant old oaks.

"No luck, I see," Frank shouts at me.

When the ringing in my ears subsides, I detect a faint meow. I need to play it cool.

"Seems like we've had the same amount of luck," I say, matching his tone.

"I'm getting close," he yells. I hope he doesn't scare Peaches off with his booming voice.

I walk along the path to catch up to him. "What do you say we call a truce and split the reward? We could work together since we're both in the woods," I suggest.

"No way. You can take your turn in the woods when I'm finished. Unless you're not confident in your detective skills." He smiles like a shrew.

When I don't respond, he shakes his head and walks in the opposite direction. My plan worked perfectly. Now I can investigate the cat cry without that busybody lurking around. I wait until he is on the other side of the park to be safe.

"Here, kitty, kitty," I whisper. "Here, kitty, kitty." I wait and listen. The tiny meow appears to be coming from the edge of the woods several yards away. I slowly walk closer.

"Here, kitty, kitty." The return meow is louder.

Stepping into the wooded area, I gaze up into the massive trees, praying Peaches isn't in one. I would never be able to reach him without help. As I peer up, I stumble and almost fall, grabbing a branch for balance. Next to my foot is a live trap with Peaches inside. I grasp the handle and walk over to Frank as fast as my old hips will carry me.

"Guess who just made seventy dollars?" I hold the cage up for him to look inside. The expression on his face is almost worth more than the reward. "Better get this little guy home. Want to pay up now, or shall I swing by later?" I try to hide my smile as Frank slowly pulls his wallet out of his pocket and hands me a twenty.

We walk the rest of the way to Peaches' house in silence. Frank rings the doorbell.

"Look who Wally and I found," he yells when the elderly neighbor opens the door. "He stumbled into one of the traps the parks and recreation folks must have set for the rabid raccoons," he continues blabbing as I set the cage down and release Peaches to his happy owner.

"Oh, I am so happy. You worried me sick, my precious Peaches," she says sternly, then covers him in kisses. "Here's the reward money for our heroes," she says, holding an envelope out to Frank.

"I'll take that," I shout a little too loudly, grabbing the envelope.

"Thank you both so much. Yesterday was miserable without my sweet baby," the happy owner says.

"Glad we could help," Frank sticks his chest out a little more. I allow him to take most of the credit. After all, the reward money and his money are all mine.

I return the trap to the edge of the woods and reset it for the city, hoping the empty tuna can will continue to work as bait for the raccoons. Satisfied with my work, I head to the store and walk straight to the lotto counter.

"Well, look what the cat drug in. So, you are feeling lucky," Fran greets me.

"I rescued Peaches. That was skill. Now, I'm hoping for some lucky scratch-offs." I smile broadly.

Fran returns a smile. "Good for you. I am so glad you found that sweet cat."

"I'll take four of the five-dollar scratchers, please. You pick," I say and slide the twenty I won from Frank across the counter.

She turns to choose and returns with four cards. "Good luck sweetie."

I'm grinning from ear to ear as I head back to sit on the bench where I saw Frank several hours earlier. The first two cards are what I like to call defective, but the third one is a thirty-dollar winner. This day keeps getting better. It doesn't even matter that the fourth is defective. I am ahead. I tuck the winner in my wallet and throw the losers in the trash can next to the bench. I can't wait to tell Martha about my exciting day. Well, at least about part of my exciting day.

9

Fran

In all my years, I never imagined I would be living in a small town, working at the lotto counter of the local grocery store. Sometimes life just happens to you. I wasn't searching for love when I decided to vacation in a tropical location. I hoped to recover from years of living in a city and dealing with privileged stuck-up kids. After twenty years of teaching Greek literature at the university, I knew it was time for a change. The university board eagerly agreed after a video surfaced of me asking one of the spoiled brats to at least use her brain for something other than a placeholder for her horrendous hat. The video went viral.

In my defense, she was dumber than a box of rocks. The only reason the university accepted her in the first place was that her grandfather's name was on the front of the building I was lecturing in. Plus, almost the entire internet agreed with me that her hat was hideous. And lastly, let's face it; there is no reason to study Greek literature. With encouragement from my therapist, I planned a vacation to clear my mind and decide what to do next.

At the airport, I picked up the trashiest novel I could find, bought a humongous hat at the resort gift shop, filled my water bottle with sparkling white wine, and made my home on the beach. During my second day of baking in the sun, a woman came over and asked if I wanted some company. As the words "no thank you" automatically came out of my mouth, I glanced up from my book. My grumpy heart melted when I saw her looking at me expectantly with a stunning smile. Her smile caught me; however, her personality made me fall for her.

My decision to move in with Susan felt reckless, but she made living in a small town, working at a grocery store, sound like the best life imaginable. At first, I didn't plan to work at the store because I was going to write the next great American novel. After staring out the window studying my new neighbors and talking to my cat for two months, I became what Susan called a bit depressed.

She suggested I come work at the store for a change of scenery. We could spend more time together, and I could study the shoppers and turn them into characters in my book. That was five years ago. So far, I haven't written anything, but I do love spending every day with Susan.

10

Martha

The birds chirping outside the window wake me from my peaceful slumber. When I glance at the clock, I can't believe an hour has passed since I laid down. I jump up to straighten the bed. When I'm satisfied, I head to the kitchen.

What to make for dinner? I forgot to take something out of the freezer this morning. The quick thaw method is a proven winner in these situations. I grab a package of pork chops and throw them in the sink filled with scalding water.

Next, I tidy up the kitchen and run to the basement to throw a load of towels in the washing machine. As soon as I reach the top step, the back door opens, and Walter practically dances into the room.

"I found Peaches! Frank was searching too, but I found him," he sings. "He was in one of those live traps the city must have set to catch the rabid raccoons attacking the neighborhood's tiny dogs." The joy on his face makes him appear ten years younger.

"I am so happy for you." On my tiptoes, I kiss his cheek and wrap my arms around his stomach. With a few extra inches around his middle, we fit differently from when we were younger.

"How was your day? Did you miss me?" he asks expectantly, pulling away from the embrace.

"I didn't have much time to miss you. I was busy with the housework." I lie.

"Did you make dinner plans? I thought I would take my best girl out to celebrate." He smiles broadly.

"That sounds lovely. I planned to make pork chops, but we can eat those tomorrow." I put the package of still-frozen meat in the fridge.

In the bathroom, I run a comb through my straight, shoulder-length bob. The same style I've worn since the boys were young. It's easy and looks good with the silver strands covering most of my head. I peruse the clothes in my closet and decide on the floral summer dress I save for special occasions. A check in the mirror reminds me how much I like to dress up, and I'm delighted the dress still fits perfectly.

Walter picks the little Italian place in the center of town. The summer evening is lovely, and people fill the streets. We have to park two blocks away. Walter takes a picture of the parking spot and the street name sign. He lost the car one day, and since then, he never leaves without taking a picture. I think it's cute how he worries. Plus, I can flip through his photos and remember all the places we visit or at least the parking spots of all the places we visit.

The stroll to the restaurant is pleasant—my dress sways in the gentle breeze. Walter takes my hand in his, bringing a smile to my face. As we pass the shop windows, I glance at our reflection. Some might say we seem like an odd pairing considering our height difference, but we fit together perfectly. Even though Walter has gained a little weight and lost some hair over the years, he is active and primarily healthy, which matters most.

After we are seated at a cozy table for two, Walter fills me in on his day. The opportunity to talk about something different from the weather is a welcome change. I am reminded of when we both held jobs and discussed interesting things. He would tell me about what those crazy kids were trying to steal at the mall. I would tell him about the parents we sent to collections because they decided not to pay for their kids' braces long after the orthodontist removed them.

I decided then and there to find something to do on my own. The community center class schedule arrived last week. It would be beneficial if we both had a few separate interests. Yes, this is an excellent idea, I think to myself, and then I realize Walter is smiling at me, not talking anymore.

"That sounds wonderful, dear. I'm so proud of you," I guess at a response.

From the expression on Walter's face, this was the correct thing to say. A passer-by might think he'd won the lotto. My turn. "I'm thinking about taking a painting class at the community center. Do you want to take it with me?" Why did I ask? I hold my breath, praying he'll say no.

He takes a bite of his warm roll before replying, "I can if you don't want to take it alone."

Always the gentleman, besides talking with his mouth full.

"You are sweet to offer, but there is no point in paying for a class you don't want to take." I try not to smile. Walter definitely won't want to take the class when I bring up the money. He's what I like to call thrifty.

"Okay, my dear," he agrees, stuffing the rest of his roll into his mouth.

Dinner is outstanding. The meal isn't anything special, but it's a treat for someone else to cook and clean up afterward. I tried to come up with something to do after dinner but couldn't think of anything. Walter won't want to spend more money when we have perfectly good, already paid-for entertainment at home—a beloved television.

I hand Walter the remote when we've settled on the couch in the family room. His eyes light up, and I make a mental note to let him choose the program more often.

At nine-thirty, he says he's tired and heads to bed. The nap I took earlier energized me, so I decide to stay up and peruse the community center class schedule. A smile spreads across my face when I think of my soon to be alone time.

11

Journal

Hold your horses and quit with the judgment. Peaches was found safe and sound. In less than a day, that rascal was back home. Not his home, mind you. He was back stalking the neighborhood. I would have thought his owners had the sense to keep him home for at least twenty-four hours to celebrate his return. Heck no. That very night he was back running the streets. Get this, though. He avoided my house like the plague. I saw him right by the neighbor's front door, but he went out on the road to cross in front of my house and then back across to my other neighbor's front door. He learned his lesson, after all. Now my sweet Sprinkles is the queen of her castle and can get the rest she deserves.

Seeing that awful cat wasn't the only terrible thing I saw that day. Right over yonder, that snotty girl, Cassie, was talking to sweet little Grace. I heard her with my own two ears. Cassie called Grace stupid and told her she couldn't ride a big girl's bike. Then Cassie told Grace she would get her a baby bottle because she was a teeny tiny baby.

Little Grace sat right down on the grass and started crying. Mind you, Cassie had just learned how to ride a bike with no training wheels this year, and she is two years older than Grace.

Cassie's mama came over and asked Cassie what had happened. The ragamuffin pouted and said she didn't know and that maybe one of the other kids was being mean to Grace. The ding-a-ling believed her! She walked over to Grace and asked which kid had been mean to her. The little piece of rubbish Cassie stood behind her mama and balled her hand in a fist and held it up in the air. Grace didn't say a word, got up, and walked home. Sad as a puppy in a rainstorm. I heard that woman thank her little brat for being a good friend and telling the truth. Telling the truth, my ass. I had never heard so many lies.

I tell you what stupid replacement for my "needs a break" therapist—I was fit to be tied. Something had to be done. How could I let Cassie get away with being so vile? What could I do? Telling her mama wasn't an option. The one time I posted on the Facebook group that one of them holier than thou prisses' sons peed in my yard, I was turned into a laughingstock.

Thankfully, the best idea popped into my head a few minutes later. I couldn't discipline that brat, but the big guy who's always watching certainly could. Not God, you silly mongoose, Santa.

I ran to the old desk in the corner and searched for the Christmas stationery from the holiday update letters I send out every Christmas. I had three pieces left. Perfect. One for the brat, one for the sweet angel, and one in case I messed up.

I put the paper in the printer and then plucked away at the keyboard, trying my darndest to sound like the big guy himself.

Mr. Santa Claus
North Pole

Dear Cassie,

You probably know that Christmas is over six months away. You might not know we started our NAUGHTY and nice list last week. There is much to do to be sure everyone is on the correct list. We are making our list and checking it twice, trying to find out who's NAUGHTY and nice. I got a couple of reports saying you're being very naughty. Hopefully, these reports are not accurate. I will watch carefully to see which list to put your name on. Maybe you can make it to the nice list before it's too late. We are inventing super cool new toys this year for all the good boys and girls and special candy too.

Some suggestions to get on the nice list include:

> Share your toys
> Never call names
> Don't lie to your mama
> Say sorry to all the kids you made cry.

I hope I can visit on Christmas Eve.

Love, Santa

Mr. Santa Claus
North Pole

My Dearest Grace,

Mrs. Claus and I are so excited about Christmas. Even though Christmas is six months away, we are making our list and checking it twice, trying to find out who is naughty and NICE.

Our reports show that you are on the extra nice list. You also made it to the really smart kid list. We are so proud of you. Keep up the excellent work.

I will be at your house on Christmas Eve with special new toys and treats we only give the nicest and smartest little kids.

Love, Santa

With both letters printed, I erased the evidence and slipped them into the envelopes. I wet the seal with tap water and wrote their names on the envelope with my left hand, all the while thinking about how smart I was.

The next thing to do was find a disguise. In the basement, I found a bin of old clothes tucked in the corner. I pulled out a black hoodie with a crow on the front. It would do. My letters slid perfectly into the front pouch. The hall closet by the front door was the best place to stash my disguise until dark when I could sneak out.

The time ticked away slower than molasses. When I was sure it was late enough, I pulled the hoodie over my head. In the hall mirror, I saw an image of my thirteen-year-old self staring back at me. My posture and build always made me appear younger than my years.

Putting those letters in the mailboxes had me sweating like a sinner in church. I reckon it wasn't just because of the warm night. But my entire body buzzed with energy on the walk home. I wish I could see Cassie's face when she reads that letter. Better yet, maybe her good-for-nothing parents will read the letter and realize what a brat they're raising. Maybe, just maybe, she'll straighten up. Do you know what journal? I do feel better. Writing this down helps me see all the good I'm doing in black and white. I think my therapist would be proud of me. She's the one who told me not to be afraid to take action.

12

Walter

Freshly brewed coffee greets my nose as I walk down the stairs. Even in retirement, Martha's an early riser. She sits on the couch, legs neatly crossed, still slender after all these years. She holds the community center class catalog up to her face with one hand and a piece of toast in the other. I guess she's allowed to break her rule of not eating on the furniture.

"Do you need anything from town today?" I ask. "I was thinking of going into the police station and joining the volunteer task force program."

"Could you get some milk and bread?" she asks, not looking up. "You can grab the twenty from my wallet in my purse. What made you want to join that program?" She glances at me over the top of her readers.

"I saw so much of the community yesterday that I realized keeping this neighborhood safe is a top priority."

"I'm happy for you, dear. It's nice to see you motivated to give back." She pushes her readers up and returns to staring at the catalog.

I take a bite of the egg white veggie scramble Martha left for me. Cold. I throw the rest in the trash and pour coffee into my to-go cup.

A quick stop at the senior center for a couple of cream-filled donuts completes my breakfast. Five minutes later, I pull the Buick into a shady spot at the police station.

A friendly young officer greets me by name as I walk in the door. Everyone here knows me, not because of anything I did wrong, mind you. I would have been an officer if it weren't for my severe color blindness. My dream ended with a strange picture of dots. Everyone but me could spot the boat. So I had to settle on protecting the mall. It wasn't bad, the pay and the hours were good, and with Martha working too, we made a nice life for ourselves and the boys. Plus, I can protect my community even in retirement with all the skills I learned.

"What can I assist you with today?" the officer asks in a friendly tone.

"Good morning. I was thinking about joining the community task force."

"We would love to have you. Frank Jones runs the community program. Even though he is retired from the force, he stays very involved in our community," she tells me in her high-pitched voice.

My mood sinks. Of course, Frank would be the one running the program.

Sensing my disappointment, she exclaims, "Your timing is perfect! We scheduled a four-hour training session next week. We want to be ready for the rise in summer crime. When those high school kids aren't in school, we need all the help we can get," she informs me in a serious tone.

I nod my head knowingly. If anyone understands delinquents,

it's me.

"If you want to fill out the application, I can enter your information into the system for the training?" her voice rises, making her statement sound more like a question.

Four hours of listening to Frank make himself sound important. Is it worth it? If I can bring up the fact that I solved the Peaches case right under his nose, it might not be so bad. Plus, my community needs me. I agree to fill out the application.

"Here you go." She slides a piece of paper and pen across the counter. "After you fill this out, we can grab your fingerprints. We don't want criminals joining the program to infiltrate the police force," she tells me in all seriousness.

My next stop is the lotto counter. As I walk to the counter, it feels like a swarm of butterflies is in my stomach. I'm unsure if the culprit is my chance at more winners or because of Fran's smile when she greets me.

"Good morning, darlin'. Goodness gracious, two days in a row. Now I'm the lucky one."

I certainly hope my cheeks don't look as red as they feel.

She takes my card and scans it into the machine. "Wow! A thirty-dollar winner. How would you like your cash?" Fran asks sweetly.

"Six five-dollar scratchers, please. You pick. You're my lucky charm."

Before sitting on the bench next to the gumball machines, I dig in my pocket for a coin. Pulling out a shiny dime, I plop down and start scratching. The first three are defective. My mood hits the floor with a sense of panic rising in my gut. The fourth reveals another loser. Not even a dollar. The odds are not with me as I uncover the fifth loser.

Taking a deep breath, I begin on the last ticket. The bingo cards take a while to scratch, but the payout can be enormous if it's a winner. I only have one number left to scratch, which needs to match at least one of the empty spots. Damn it. Defective. I throw all the cards in the trash bin and slowly walk towards the dairy section, not believing my lousy luck.

"Any winners?" Fran calls out.

"Not today."

"Well, doggone it. I'm sorry, hon. Maybe next time."

She is so sweet.

The organic milk Martha insists on has a sale tag below the regular price. Two dollars off, my luck is improving. Now to locate the fancy bread she likes. In the front sits one loaf with a half-off sticker. The expiration date was yesterday, but the regular six-dollar price is now three dollars. Yes, it will mold faster. However, I can suggest sandwiches for dinner, and with a bit of sweet talk, Martha might make her famous french toast for breakfast. A break from the egg white scramble would be fantastic. My step is a little lighter as I walk to the front of the store to pay. My luck has returned. I slide most of the change into my front pocket, telling myself Martha will never be the wiser if I buy one more scratcher. And really, how can I not?

I lay a five-dollar bill on the lotto counter, "One more, you pick."

"I feel good about this one," Fran tells me, handing me one of the special edition Easy Money cards.

Beads of sweat form on my forehead as I walk to my car. Summer in North Carolina is either hot or unbearably hot. The car's AC started acting up this morning, so there's no point in starting the car up yet. But even with the windows down, I'll need to scratch quickly so the milk doesn't spoil.

First, I remove the label from the day-old bread. I fold the sticky part on itself and push it into my pocket. Now it's time to scratch. All I need to do is match the lucky number to any of the numbers below. I grab a penny from my cup holder and reveal my lucky number. Seventeen. I scratch off each number one at a time.

Fifteen, twenty-seven, three, eighteen, sixteen, why do they do this to me? I wipe the sweat off my forehead with the back of my hand before scratching the last number. Seventeen! I matched! I slowly scrape off the coating to reveal the prize beneath—only a five-dollar winner. At least I'm back in the game. I touch the milk carton. It's already getting warm. My winning ticket will have to wait. I shove the card into my pocket and drive the short distance home.

13

Martha

Last night, after Walter went to bed, I read every entry in the community center catalog, including the description of the preschool swim classes. I wanted to make the right decision. Most people sign up and don't give it a second thought. Not me, though. Money on a fixed income is always a little tight, and I won't waste it on a class I wouldn't enjoy or at least learn something.

My head was spinning with all the information, so I decided a walk would do me good. Walking is my favorite way to exercise but not in the middle of the day during the summer. Too hot. Last night was perfect; there was even a slight breeze. Later, when I climbed into bed, I fell asleep with a clear head.

Over my second cup of coffee this morning, I narrowed my choices down to a watercolor and a self-defense class for seniors.

The watercolor class is held two mornings a week in the park, weather permitting. The cost is sixty dollars but includes supplies. I can walk to the park, meaning I wouldn't need to bother Walter for rides or leave him without a car. I allowed myself a moment to daydream about two hours a week to be creative.

The self-defense class would be held on four Saturdays from nine to noon starting this week and would be a good idea for several reasons. For one, parking lots make me jumpy when I'm by myself. I blame *Dateline*. Some defensive skills would help my confidence when I go out without Walter. Secondly, my physical health is essential, and I like to keep my muscles active. With all the kicking and hitting involved, the workout alone offers more than my usual walks.

The cost is one hundred dollars, which is a lot of money, but what is my safety and peace of mind worth? Walter most likely wouldn't be interested in taking the class with me. He prides himself on the self-defense skills he learned through the training he did for his job protecting the citizens at the mall. On the other hand, he would enjoy showing off those skills to everyone, including the instructor, which would make me crazy. I don't like show-offs. How I word this will be important. I'll wait until after lunch. If I make him the fancy grilled ham and cheese sandwich he likes, he'll be more willing to spend the money. Walter walks into the kitchen just as I finish tidying up.

"Hello dear, how did it go?" I ask and make an effort to greet him with a hug. Desperate times call for desperate measures.

He sets the bread and milk on the counter. "Fine and dandy."

"Must be a hot one today," I tell him when I grab the milk to put it in the fridge.

"Uh-huh." He's distracted. I'll use this to my advantage.

"You go watch the news. I'll make lunch. Thank you for buying my favorite bread."

Even though he annoys me sometimes, he is thoughtful.

The news clicks on in the living room, and I get busy making the perfect sandwich. Still hot from the griddle, I quickly put the sandwich and his favorite dill pickles on a plate. When I set it on his lap, he looks at me like this is a test.

"I thought you hated when I ate in the living room." Walter stares at the plate, then back at me.

"No worries, dear. I need to vacuum anyway," I assure him. "The news looks exciting today," I add, sitting beside him.

During a commercial break, he asks if I have decided on a class. Here's my chance.

"I found two that sound interesting, but I'm not sure we can afford them. The first is a watercolor class in the park. The cost is sixty dollars but includes all the supplies. The class meets twice a week for eight weeks, which is good value for the money. Supplies alone probably cost fifty dollars."

I don't wait for him to respond before continuing, "I was also thinking about a self-defense class for seniors. A retired Navy SEAL teaches it. Supporting our military and keeping me safe is worth the one hundred dollar fee." I quit rambling and wait for him to respond.

Walter takes a bite of his sandwich and says, "I could teach you some safety tactics or go everywhere with you. My most important job is to keep you safe."

I knew he would need some persuading. "You do a great job. Over forty years with no incidents. How about if I see what the class has to offer? I can get a full refund if I don't like it."

His brow furrows as he stares into space—his thinking face.

"We could pull money from the Christmas savings account," he offers. "The only thing I need for Christmas is you safe and sound, and God knows our boys don't need anything they can't buy on their own. Then you could take both classes, and I could make a few home improvements. Maybe there will even be a little money left over. Some extra spending money this summer could be fun," he grins at me.

Well, this is a pleasant surprise. I almost ask, who are you, and what have you done with my husband? But I think better of it and decide to enjoy my good fortune.

"That sounds wonderful. What improvements were you thinking of making?" I ask.

"I noticed several sections of the fence have rotted. I estimate the cost to replace them will be about five hundred dollars. And the bathroom faucet has been leaking. Replacing that will most likely lower our water bill. I can even bring the car in to have the air serviced. Yesterday it was blowing lukewarm air at best, and that won't do with this heat."

"All splendid ideas, dear." I am giddy.

After I bring the empty plate into the kitchen, I call the community center to sign up for both classes. It doesn't even bother me when I have to drag the vacuum out to clean up Walter's mess.

14

Walter

My favorite cargo shorts are right where I left them. The old chair Martha insisted on having in the bedroom is the perfect place to keep my clothes. No sense in hanging them up if I'm going to wear them again the next day.

Martha has my travel coffee mug filled and ready to go. A healthy breakfast bar, she insists tastes good, sits next to my coffee, making this a good day to stop by the senior center.

Raspberry-filled donuts—hot diggity dog. I pull the breakfast bar from my pocket and toss it in the trash can before grabbing two donuts—one for each hand. I finish them in the parking lot walking back to my car. After licking my fingers clean, I wipe them on my shorts and head to the bank.

The line is five people deep. When I'm finally first, I recognize my favorite teller and cross my fingers that the timing is right. She finishes up with her customer and calls me over. My luck continues.

"Good morning, Walter. What can I do for you?"

"Good morning, Olivia. I want to pull one thousand dollars from our Christmas saving account." I slide my driver's license across the counter.

"You're a bit early this year. Are you having a Christmas in July celebration?" she asks warmly.

"We will be if Santa brings me a new fence and fixes the AC in the car," I chuckle.

"I'm not sure he can fit a fence in his sleigh or if he's a licensed mechanic, but I'll put in a good word for you if he comes into the bank. I hope you've been a good boy." She gives me a wink.

Is it getting hot in here? When she turns to retrieve the money, I grab a brochure off the display rack and casually fan my face. She slips my cash into a bank envelope, and I hurry to the car. This much money at once makes me nervous. I put ten twenty-dollar bills in my wallet to pay for Martha's classes. The rest goes in the glove box.

My next stop is the community center. I am so proud of Martha for trying new things. She can make Christmas presents this year in her watercolor class, and I won't need to take out more money in December. The thought of the boys opening up original artwork instead of the fancy things Martha usually insists on buying them makes me smile.

After paying for Martha's classes, I head to the lumber yard. The price of fencing is a lot more than I remember. And the faucets must be made of pure gold with how much they want for them. I'm scared to find out how much it will cost to fix the air in the car. That will need to go on the maybe list while I shop for a cheaper faucet and fencing. Money sure doesn't go as far as it used to. It might be time for a trip to the casino.

One last stop to turn in my winning scratcher.

"Good morning, hon. Three days in a row, you must be on a lucky streak," Fran greets me with her beautiful smile.

"I have a winner." When I pull the ticket from my pocket, the bread sticker flies out and lands on the counter.

"Is someone pricing their own bread?" she teases me.

My cheeks grow hot and are probably bright red. I hope Fran doesn't notice. "Nope, just keeping my thrift shopping from the missus. I don't want to let on how cheap I am." I chuckle as I pick up the sticker and stuff it in my pocket.

"Do you want me to cash this in for you today?"

"No, I think I'll take another scratcher. Better yet, make it five," I say, fumbling to pull a twenty from my wallet. "You pick. You're my lucky charm."

She picks five cards and hands them to me with a smile. "I hope they are all winners."

"Thank you." I turn and hurry to my car.

After rolling every single window down, I start scratching. The first four are defective. Thank God I win ten dollars on the fifth card. I'm still in the game, but a big win with these scratchers is not looking good. I shove the winner in my pocket and drive to the store entrance to throw the losers in the trash can.

I decide to put two one hundred dollar bills from the bank envelope into my wallet. Hopefully, Martha won't count the money, and she'll be none the wiser until I can replace it after a big win at the casino.

I slide the money envelope into my back pocket when I arrive home. My plan to use the kitchen door to avoid Martha backfires. She's sitting at the kitchen table with a glass of iced tea and her nose in a book. I breeze past her and head straight for the living room.

"I paid for your classes," I say over my shoulder. "I'll put the rest of the cash in the desk drawer." I open the secret drawer and slide the envelope in, praying she won't ask to count the money.

"Thank you for paying for my classes, dear. You can take the car this Saturday after you drop me off at the community center."

"That sounds like a good plan. I could get a jump start on the fence project."

"We need to run to the grocery store. Remember, when we shopped earlier this week, the black beans were out of stock, and I need a couple of other things," Martha informs me.

As we walk into the store a half-hour later, Fran calls out, "Nice to see you again. Did you have any winners?"

"My wife is my only winner," I say, my eyebrows rising. She mouths 'sorry' as Martha turns to go down the produce aisle.

"What is she talking about?" Martha asks when I catch up to her.

"I have no idea. She must be confused. We old people all look alike," I chuckle, hoping it doesn't come across as nervous.

The grocery total comes to eighteen dollars and some change. The cashier hands me a dollar bill and several coins.

"Do you want a scratcher?" Martha asks before I put the dollar in my wallet.

"No, I'm not really into scratchers anymore."

"I will remember that at Christmas time."

"I might change my mind, but I have the only winner I need right now." I kiss her cheek and wave to Fran from behind Martha's back on the way out.

15

Journal

Those letters from Santa worked. Since then, that brat Cassie's been acting sweet as molasses. I saw her give little Grace her stuffed monkey. Grace was so happy she ran all over the yard with it. Cassie kept staring at the sky as if Santa was spying on her from outer space. Kids can be so stupid.

16

Martha

I'm the first to arrive at the self-defense class. The folding chairs form a circle in the community center's gymnasium. "First come, first served," I whisper and choose a chair facing the doors.

While waiting for the others to arrive, I check my phone to appear busy. Five minutes before class is supposed to start, two older women come in and sit two chairs away from me. They are having an animated discussion and appear to be friends. Next, an older gentleman enters and sits facing me, his back to the door. A woman with red hair, followed by a young lady who appears to be a teenager, arrives next.

The woman sits next to me and introduces herself. "Hi there, I'm Julie, and this is my granddaughter Jolynn. We're gonna learn self-defense together, ain't that right, dear?" she says with a thick drawl.

The girl grunts and continues to stare at her phone, already bored.

The class was in the fifty-five and older section of the community catalog. That was one of the reasons I took it. I didn't sign up to hang around unrelatable teens. I smile at the woman to hide my true feelings. If the class ends up being terrible, I can use her bored teen as my excuse to ask for a refund.

A few more people show up and fill all but one of the empty chairs. The instructor walks in ten minutes late—one more reason for a refund.

"Sorry for the delay. I was trying to print my class list, and as you can see, I don't have it, so that did not go well." He grabs the empty chair and flips it around, causing the legs to screech across the floor. "Let's begin and learn who everyone is together." He straddles the chair with his bravado and lack of manners on full display.

"I will begin. My name is Titus. I am a Navy SEAL. Once a SEAL, always a SEAL. I worked as a secret service agent for ten years and as an FBI agent for another ten years. Now I go around the country teaching self-defense and martial arts. If you want to check out my popular YouTube channel, it is titled, *The Only Easy Day Was Yesterday.*" Titus takes a moment to meet eyes with every person in the circle. He stops on the young lady sitting next to Julie.

"This is a self-defense class for seniors. Are you a senior in high school?" he asks the teen staring at her phone.

She glances up but doesn't say a word.

"The office said we could take the class together," Julie sputters.

"Alrighty then, this will be a class for seniors, as in anyone above fifty-five and one senior in high school." He claps his hands together and smirks.

I like him and forgive him for his tardiness and lack of manners.

"There are two kinds of people that take this class. First are the people who want to learn how to defend themselves. Second are the people who want to learn how to become better criminals. My job is to supply both groups with tips and strategies to stay safe or not get caught. You decide if you will use this class for good or evil." He smiles, showing off his perfectly straight, extremely white teeth. "Let's go around the room to introduce ourselves. Say your name and which group you fall into." He turns to Julie. "We will start with you. Are you here to learn self-defense, or are you and your high school senior considering starting a crime family?"

"We're here for self-defense," Julie answers in a tight voice.

He goes around the circle; everyone says their name and states they are here to learn self-defense.

"Last chance to have a criminal in our midst. Please introduce yourself and your purpose," he says, looking directly into my eyes.

"I am Martha. I would love to say I am here to jump-start my life's second act and begin my life of crime, but I, too, am here for self-defense training." He winks at me. I quickly look at my lap, hoping my face isn't as red as it feels.

"Today, we will set the groundwork for the other classes. The first and most important tip in self-defense is to be aware of your surroundings. Who do you think is sitting in the best seat?" Titus asks the group.

The man across from me speaks up, "I think I am. I'm closest to the door, so I will be the first one out of here if anything goes wrong."

"You are actually in the worst spot," Titus informs him. "According to your logic, you would have to run past the perpetrator to reach an exit. You would also be the last person to see what is happening if anyone walked in the door ready to harm us."

A couple of the others think their seats are the best. Titus tells all of them that they are wrong and points to me.

"Martha sat in the best seat. She can monitor the entire area and has the best view of the door and emergency exits. She could be up and out of her seat, running for the side exit before Ms. High School Senior looks up from her phone," He claps his hands together sharply, making me jump. "Now, let's all go outside to play a game I call assailant hide-and-seek. The goal is to maintain a safety bubble by identifying threats and being aware of your surroundings at all times."

The game gets my blood pumping as I call out possible attack points. Julie screams when I run out of the bushes and startle her. I cross my legs to avoid having an accident as I stifle my laughter.

Next, we practice throwing a purse or a set of keys. One student yells, "I have a gun. Give me your purse." The other student throws the purse or keys as far as possible and runs in the opposite direction. I'm out of breath when we return to the gym for a water break.

"Okay, folks," Titus says as everyone settles back into their chair. "Which body part is your best weapon?"

"My arms," a man guesses, flexing his tiny, aged arm.

"Nope, does anyone else have a guess?" Titus asks.

"My legs," a woman says, stretching out her long leg.

"Nope, that is your second-best weapon. DOES ANYONE ELSE HAVE A GUESS?" Titus bellows.

"Your voice," I yell. I love being correct, even if that makes me the teacher's pet.

"Correct. Screaming into someone's ear can cause a great deal of discomfort and has the benefit of grabbing other people's attention. Most of the time, you don't need to overtake an attacker; you only need to startle them to escape and obtain help."

We practice yelling "stop" and "help" as we walk around the gym. At first, I'm timid, but by the end, I'm shouting at the top of my lungs. This class has invigorated me.

"Exceptional job today, Martha. You have incredible instincts. You might want to reconsider starting your life of crime." Titus grins at me.

"Thanks, I will give it some thought." I laugh, hoping he thinks I'm flushed because of all the activity.

17

Walter

After dropping Martha at the community center's doors, I head to the senior center for breakfast. Only plain fried cakes today, but that's okay. I'm saving my luck for the casino. I smile when I think of the two hundred dollars from the Christmas account sitting in my wallet. Merry Christmas to me.

With a thirty-minute drive there and back, I'm left with two hours to double or triple my money. If I win right away, I'll treat myself to the buffet. My mouth waters at the thought of eating all the foods Martha doesn't allow in my diet.

The main lot has plenty of parking spaces when I pull in. I snap a quick picture of the lot marker with my phone. Today would be a bad day to lose the car. I don't have time for that.

My adrenaline goes into high gear as soon as I step into the casino. Stale smoke greets my nose, and my ears dance with the hoots and hollers of people winning. The last time I set foot in the casino was when my extravagant cousin and his wife visited from California years ago. We ran out of things to do by the second day. Martha was worried they would think we were boring, small-town people, so I suggested the casino, promising Martha that I wouldn't gamble. The buffet was surprisingly good, making it a little easier to swallow the fact that I couldn't join in the fun at the poker tables with my cousin. I have really missed this place.

I walk around the smoky room of mesmerized players hunting for a hot machine. I find one of my favorites from back in the day when I was a regular. All I need is a good line hit or six golden nuggets to trigger the bonus game. I slide into the seat and insert a crisp one hundred dollar bill, quietly saying a prayer.

The first two spins are a bust. Down ten dollars in less than sixty seconds. I should lower my bet, but my wins probably won't be as significant. The next spin is looking good, but nothing lines up perfectly. My rule is that if I lose four in a row, I move to a different machine. I push the button and close my eyes. Please let it hit. The bells ring, and my eyes pop open—a twenty-five dollar win! I break even on the next spin, but my next four are a bust—time to find a better machine.

At this rate, the buffet isn't going to be an option. Maybe the poker slots will be hot. A full house in the first round means a winning hand. The next four are losers.

I wander around for a few minutes, searching for a hot machine. Fortune Coin sounds lucky, and the game is easy to understand. Two free spin symbols pop up on my first spin—please give me one more.

Yes! Five free spins.

Nothing lines up until my last free spin. A winner! Ten dollars! Although, I was hoping for better than that. The next four spins are losers—time to move. When the ticket spits out of the machine, I do the math and realize I am down almost sixty-eight dollars. How did that happen in less than thirty minutes? Something needs to change and fast.

I cash out my voucher and head over to the ten-dollar blackjack tables. The greasy-haired dealer takes the cash I lay on the table and hands me six five-dollar chips. I push two chips onto the betting circle and hold my breath.

My first two cards are aces. Smart players always split aces and eights, so I do. With the split, you have two winning hands instead of one. I'm dealt a nine on the first hand, giving me twenty. I stay.

I'm dealt a five on my second hand. Not ideal, but the dealer is showing an eight, so I assume he has at least an eighteen. I need to hit. The dealer flips over a six—worse than before. I motion for one more card. A jack. Bust. I silently pray the twenty will hold.

The dealer turns over his card—a three. He takes the next card—a queen. Twenty-one. Damn it. I can only play one more hand.

My first card is a nine. The second is a four. Hit. My next card is a ten. Bust.

Back to the slots it is. 88 Fortunes has a five thousand dollar jackpot, so I slide my last one hundred dollar bill into the machine and decide on max bet spins. I need to ensure my chance to win the jackpot.

First spin. Nothing. I push the button again to reveal another loser. I still feel good about this one, but I won't go below fifty dollars.

Another push. Another loss.

My stomach is tied in a knot. I need to turn this around.

Three more spins—three more losses. I broke my rule of no more than four spins on a losing machine. Damn it. The machine spits out my voucher, showing I only have forty-six dollars and seventy-two cents.

I glance at my watch. Forty-five minutes until I need to pick

Martha up. I slide the voucher into the machine on the aisle. They say the aisle machines usually have more wins. Five minutes later, I'm left with thirty-two cents, blowing that theory.

With no cash in my wallet, it's time to go. I need to pick up Martha anyway. My mind races, and I have to look at the darn picture on my phone three times before I find my car.

Time to formulate a new plan. If I'm frugal with the repairs, everything will turn out okay. Martha won't ever know I made a trip to the casino. I drive with the windows down, hoping to rid my clothes of the cigarette smoke that clings to every fiber. At the stoplight, I grab the bottle of vanilla hand sanitizer Martha keeps in the car and rub it on both of my arms. Now I stink like a burnt marshmallow.

The clock on the dash says I have ten minutes to spare as I turn the corner to the road where the community center is located. I'm not over on this side of town much, so I am pleasantly surprised when I spot a Habitat for Humanity ReStore. I slam on the brakes and turn sharply into the parking lot.

The friendly cashier directs me to the back of the store where they keep the fencing. They have several sections in decent condition, and the price is way less than what the hardware store wanted for new panels. These are weathered, not rotted like mine, but not new. Martha will notice.

A young man disturbs my thoughts, "Need some fencing?"

"Yes, but I was hoping for something a little newer."

"You can power wash these. They clean up real easy and will be as good as new in no time," he informs me, trying to make a sale.

That's not a bad idea, but I'll need to pull out the old power washer. Hopefully, it still works.

"Thanks for the tip. I'll be back for these. Where would I find bathroom sink faucets?" I ask.

He points me in the right direction. All the faucets are worse than the leaky one residing in my bathroom. No way I can pass any of these off as new. I do some calculations in my head. With the savings on the fence panels, I'll buy a new faucet and have some money left to repair the car's AC.

Everything will be alright if Martha doesn't count the money before I can replenish it.

18

Journal

That lazy therapist instructed me to get lots of exercise. Said it helps with physical and mental health. I must admit that walking has always helped me feel pretty darn good. I love getting up at the crack of dawn and walking to the library before it gets too hot. Two of my book holds were in, and I was looking forward to a relaxing weekend of sitting back with my feet up and my head in a book.

But wouldn't you know someone was trying to ruin my perfectly good day. On my walk home from the library, I almost fell over with shock when I walked back into my neighborhood. The first house (you know, the one that welcomes you into our community) had hung a giant flag from that extremist group. It was bigger than the bed of the huge pickup truck they keep in the driveway. You know, the one with those offensive naked lady mud flaps.

And if that weren't bad enough, surrounding the flag were at least ten political signs. As I live and breathe, those morons supported that good-for-nothing leader that had caused our great country to go right into the crapper. One sign said, "Make America Awesome Again," and another, "Together we can save America." I will have to look at those signs every time I leave my neighborhood until November!

My blood boiled. The way they sat near the "Welcome to the Neighborhood" sign made it appear that everybody in our entire community supported those fools. What if my relatives came to visit and thought I was one of those awful people supporting that swine?

My absent therapist would say, "Talk to them, find some common ground." I thought about giving them a piece of my mind, but what's the point? My daddy always used to say, "Common sense ain't a flower that grows in everybody's garden, and from the looks of it, they ain't got no flowers."

I stewed as I walked the rest of the way home. I tried to read my book, but I couldn't concentrate. I opened up the neighborhood Facebook page, hoping to find other people as mad as me, but there was nothing but crickets, not one word. The only thing posted was about the potluck on Thursday. The nincompoops would walk to the golf course to stare at the fireworks. Celebrating the birth of our nation by drinking and partying is not for me. No siree. I'll be sitting in my house trying to calm my sweet fur baby with a glass of sweet tea and my head in a book.

I got to thinking that maybe this year I'd get in the spirit after all and do a little firework show of my own.

19

Martha

The credits from *Dateline* roll across the screen while I work on filling in the calendar for the week:

Walter's training at the police station.

My watercolor class.

Groceries and errands.

The Fourth of July.

The neighborhood has a block party every Fourth of July, and right before sunset, everyone walks to the golf course with blankets, sparklers, and glow sticks. Our family always watched the fireworks on the green of the seventh hole. When the boys were little, we had so much fun. I loved watching them run around with their friends. During sunset, Walter would have a couple of beers he put in a koozie so that they would pass as soda. Drinking is not permitted, but everyone does anyway. Once the fireworks began, the boys would come and lay with us on the blanket, and we would snuggle, oohing and aahing at the light display.

I sure do miss the days when the boys were young. After they grew up and moved out, we stayed home to watch the fireworks from our backyard. Some years we didn't even bother. Walter said, "If you've seen one firework display, you've seen them all." And for me, it hasn't been the same without the boys.

"Busy week," I tell Walter when I show him the calendar during our usual Sunday pot roast dinner.

"Frank sent an email and asked if I would be willing to help monitor the crowd at the fireworks. We don't want a repeat of last year's nonsense when Dave yelled and screamed at his wife and son in front of the whole neighborhood until the police showed up and hauled him away," Walter says, shaking his head at the memory. "You're welcome to patrol with me if you want. I don't want my best girl to be lonely on America's birthday."

"I think I'll stay home and watch from the yard. It will be more relaxing," I assure him with a smile, secretly giddy with his news.

I envisioned skipping the boring fireworks to binge on my guilty pleasure, *Destination Dating*. All the young people go to a beach and hook up with each other. I would never tell anyone I enjoy that rubbish, not even Walter.

20

Walter

The senior center has fancy frosted Fourth of July donuts this morning. I grab three—two for now and one for later. The extra sugar will come in handy to make it through a morning with Frank. I trudge into the police station, prepared to be bored. I am already aware of everything concerning community policing, thanks to my common sense, trusty police scanner, and years of service protecting the outlet mall.

Five elderly gentlemen and one woman are sitting in the room. No one from the station bothers to offer us a drink or a snack. I would have thought my tax dollars would pay for water and a candy bar or something. An empty coffee pot sits on the back table. Frank is too self-absorbed or incompetent to have thought to brew a pot.

We listen as Frank goes on about what we can and cannot do. The presentation could have easily been broken down to the fact that we can't do anything but call for backup and document, document, document. Frank likes to hear himself talk, and boy, can he talk. He tells story after story with the same ending; he is the town's hero. I should have brought my earplugs.

The only important part is a tutorial on how the walkie-talkie works and the correct channel to call for assistance. When Frank finally stops talking, he presents each participant with an official button-up shirt and a badge. The badge says Greenville Community Officer and is surprisingly heavy. At least I got a shiny badge— Martha is sure to be impressed.

On the way home, I decided to stop at the grocery store to reward myself with some scratchers. I managed to sit through the entire training without saying one rude thing to Frank about how I found Peaches. Maybe Frank used to be a fantastic officer, but my neighbors know who the better detective is.

I walk up to the service counter, thankful to see Fran is working.

"Good afternoon, sugar. You sure have been lucky lately," she says, scanning my ticket. "A ten-dollar winner. Would you like to cash out today?"

"Nah, I think I'll take more scratchers. How about two of *America the Beautiful* in celebration of the Fourth."

"Do you have plans for the holiday?" she asks, over her shoulder, tearing off my cards from the roll.

"I am assisting local law enforcement in ensuring everyone has a good time legally," I say, pulling my badge from my pocket. Fran studies it.

"Impressive. I'm glad there are people like you in our community to keep everyone safe."

"Got to do my part. Will you be attending the fireworks?" I ask.

"I might go down to the golf course and see what trouble I can get into," she smirks.

"You get into trouble? No way. I am sure an upstanding citizen like yourself would never break any laws."

"People can be deceiving. I could be running a crime family in my spare time." She giggles.

I love her laugh.

"Inconceivable. I'm certain you're not a criminal. I can spot one a mile away. You, my dear, don't have a bad bone in your body," I insist.

"You got me. I don't even speed. I did jaywalk once, but not on purpose. I promise." She holds her hand to her heart and winks.

I'm feeling lucky as I head to the car. I grab a coin from the center console and start scratching. The first is defective, but the second is a twenty-dollar winner. I debate going back to cash it in to get four more. My banter with Fran was so much fun. However, at the moment, I can't think of any more clever things to say. If I wait to cash it in until after the Fourth, I can tell her about the crimes I prevented to keep our town safe. I shove the tickets in my pocket and drive home to impress Martha with my badge.

21

Martha

My first painting class is tomorrow morning, and my stomach is in knots thinking about it. I decide to do a little research. The last thing I want to do is look foolish. I search for famous watercolor artists on the internet and check out some YouTube videos of painting techniques. After watching several videos, I check out my self-defense instructor's YouTube channel, *The Only Easy Day Was Yesterday*. He is as funny on the screen as in person.

The garage door opens, and I snap my computer shut. Walter would think I'm wasting my time watching those videos. He is not a big fan of the internet and says the newspaper is the best source of information. I'm pretty sure there aren't any painting techniques in the newspaper.

He walks in with a big smile and holds out a shiny badge for me to admire. "How nice, honey. It almost looks real," I say, glancing at his badge.

His face sags, and I know I hurt his feelings. I didn't mean for it to come out that way. Usually, I'm better at keeping those thoughts to myself. He goes to take a nap and skips lunch. I let him rest before going upstairs to apologize and tell him what a great job he is doing for our community. He rolls out of bed, barely looking my way. He mopes while I make his favorite cake from scratch. They say, "the way to a man's heart is through his stomach." Walter has never guessed I replace the oil with sugar-free applesauce.

After dinner, I hand him the remote. He picks a superhero show where no one seems to care that one person is green and another is purple, and they can fly and stop a train with their minds. I pretend to be interested as I dream about painting in the morning. When we go to bed, I snuggle up, kiss him, and tell him how proud I am of him. I think he believes me. One of the best parts about being married for so many years is we never stay angry for long.

22

Martha

I bounce out of bed as soon as the clock clicks to six a.m. After tossing and turning all night, today will require strong coffee. The news can't even distract me from my whirling thoughts. The last time I painted was when the kids and I decorated rocks with inspirational messages. We filled our rock garden with them and left a hand-painted sign. "Take a rock—change your outlook."

It was a fun way to spread some kindness to our community. All was well until someone threw one of the rocks through the church window. Can you imagine throwing a rock that says, "Rejoice Always" through a beautiful stained-glass window at the church?

The police questioned the kids and me, but they knew we would never do such a thing. We removed the rest of the rocks from our garden. The guilt of supplying the weapon used in the crime ate me up, so I anonymously donated money so the church could fix the window.

After two cups of coffee, I am buzzing. I whip up Walter's egg white scramble. The man would starve without me. I throw in some laundry, empty the dishwasher, take out some meat for dinner, change the kitty litter, and check my email. With my work done and dusted, as my mama used to say, I decided to walk to the park a little early.

The instructor is already there frantically trying to set up. She reminds me of a female version of Bob Ross. It looks like she tried to pull her curly hair into a bun, but half of it is flying around her face. She trips as she bounces around, setting the easels back up after the wind blows them over. When I offer to help, her face lights up.

"Thank you so much. The wind is working against me. I do love nature even though sometimes it doesn't love me." She giggles a sweet little laugh as she brushes the hair out of her eyes. Even though she's a klutz, she does seem genuine, giving me hope this will be a good class.

We carefully stack all the supplies on the chairs, fill jars with water, and place one at each spot. Four women and one man slowly fill in the seats. Everyone appears to be retired, with gray hair and glasses. I'm thankful no young people are in this class.

I take a seat next to a woman who introduces herself as Bonnie. She informs me she lives on the other side of the park, pointing in the direction opposite my house. She wears a Bohemian dress with perfectly matching, one-of-a-kind jewelry. Her long, curly, gray hair has a touch of brown, and a colorful scarf ties it back loosely. She's hip without trying.

"I love our little neighborhood with this lovely park right in the center. Walking to the library and the grocery store is a bonus. I try to walk every day. I've been looking forward to this class for weeks. Don't make fun of me, but I even searched painting techniques on the Google." Bonnie finally takes a breath.

I smile and confess, "Me too."

We chat like old friends from that moment. She tells me about her three kids—two sons and a daughter. Her sons are doing well; one is married with two kids, ages four and six. Her other son and his partner recently adopted a beautiful daughter. She shows me a photo of the family all grinning from ear to ear.

"I never worry about my boys. On the other hand, my daughter keeps me up at night," Bonnie sighs.

"Why?" I ask.

"Ashley is a lovely young woman with a beautiful son, but her husband is nothing but trouble. I think he drinks too much and abuses her. She denies it, but she can't hide the bruises every time. Anytime I voice my concern, she tells me what a good man Dave is and how he provides for her and Charlie. Good man, my ass," Bonnie huffs and rolls her eyes. "She had the nerve to say that maybe I should concentrate on my own marriage. Ashley blames me for everything bad that has ever happened to her. I didn't think I did a bad job raising my kids." Bonnie stops abruptly and adds, "Oh dear, I'm talking your ears right off. Tell me about you."

My problems suddenly seem minuscule compared to what she is dealing with. I'm not sure how to address it. So I don't.

"I have two boys, both married. I'm hoping for some grandbabies soon, but they are taking their sweet time." I roll my eyes and continue, "I have been married to my husband, Walter, for over forty years. He is a good man, and I thank God for our life together, even though he drives me crazy sometimes. The other day, I walked into the living room, to find him sitting on the sofa in his underwear, eating chips right out of the bag. He said it was better because he wouldn't get crumbs on his pants or dirty a bowl." I laugh nervously, wondering if I have overshared.

Bonnie nods knowingly. I take it as a sign she understands, so I continue my story.

"Finding some of our own interests is helping. Walter recently started volunteering with the local police helping with their community policing program. He dreamt of being an officer but had to settle for being a security guard. In retirement, he can finally live his dream, and it gives him something to do."

"I completely understand. If my husband, Trevor, didn't golf twice a week and visit his mother at least once a month for several days, I think we would have killed each other long ago. He drives me nuts when he follows me around the house, asking what I'm doing every two minutes. But he's a good man, and I'm lucky too." I smile at her and nod.

"Cats or Dogs?" Bonnie blurts.

"Cats," we say in unison and giggle like school girls.

"How many?" she asks.

"I have one. How about you?"

"Me too! I wanted two, but Trevor said no. That doesn't mean I'll quit trying. I have my ways." She winks, giving me a sly smile.

Our conversation is interrupted when the instructor greets everyone. She starts with simple painting techniques—several of which I had watched on the YouTube videos. We practice making happy trees. Mine are similar to the ones in Bob Ross' paintings. And guess what? Bob was right; they do make me happy.

"Now we are going to work on our first masterpiece," the instructor says in a calming voice. "Before we start, I want us to take a moment to imagine a sunset. Close your eyes and visualize all the magnificent colors. Picture the birds and animals finishing their days and heading to bed. The cool evening breeze gently caresses your face as the day's heat dissipates. Envision the sun descending, leaving behind the night sky and the moon mother rising to protect us through the night."

"What do you think her drug of choice is?" Bonnie giggles.

I bite my tongue to keep from laughing.

We begin with a fresh canvas and a circle sticker to use as the sun or moon. The first step is adding the colors of the setting sun. Pink, reds, and oranges fill my canvas. Next, we create some trees and plants using dark colors to resemble shadows.

Bonnie leans over and whispers out of the side of her mouth, "What did you think of the political signs the neighbors put up?"

"I think they are terrible," I whisper back, hoping she agrees.

"I was so disgusted. Guess what I did when I walked by them the other day?" Bonnie giggles.

"What did you do?" I ask, eyebrows raised with my brush in mid-air.

"I spit on them. I think I hit at least three before my mouth ran dry. Sometimes I wish I was a man so I could have done worse. I would relieve myself on all kinds of offensive things. That dog that won't stop barking, and that truck with those offensive naked lady mud flaps," she laughs and continues painting.

I laugh out loud. Everyone's head turns my way, and my cheeks burn. I quickly return to my canvas, but my smile stays as I think about how Bonnie and I are so much alike.

The instructor directs us to remove the round sticker. The white circle sticks out like a sore thumb against the dark paint. Now to choose if I want it to be a moon or the setting sun.

By the time class is over, my blank canvas is transformed into a dazzling sunset. I have the perfect spot for my work of art on the guest room wall.

"I am so glad I am taking this class. I met a fabulous new friend and created a beautiful painting," Bonnie tells me as we clean up our areas.

I beam at her compliment and add, "Me too."

We help the instructor pack the easels and bring them to her car. I give Bonnie a quick hug and hand her a scrap of paper.

"Here is my cell phone number." I hope I'm not coming off too strong. "Let me know if you want Walter to ask around the station for resources for your daughter and her family."

"Thank you," she says, taking the paper. "See you later."

Bonnie walks towards my house. I thought she said she lived on the opposite side of the park from me. I could catch up and ask her, but I don't want her to think I'm a nosey neighbor. When I'm almost home, I spot Bonnie and a young woman sitting on the front porch a few houses from mine. Bonnie is right—her daughter's husband is no good.

23

Journal

My therapist said to make a to-do list to stay focused on my goals. The first thing on my list was the Shop and Save one town over to buy water bottles with squirty tops. They only had a twenty-four pack. I guess I'll be hydrated for the rest of the summer.

That bugger was so heavy I could barely get it into the cart, so I asked for help getting it to the car. As the young man loaded them into my trunk, I thought about scrapping my whole plan and going to the gas station to buy a single water bottle. But it would've cost the same as the twenty-four pack, and I didn't want to draw any attention to myself returning the ones I had already bought. Plus, doesn't everyone have water in their garage just in case the water treatment plant goes bad again?

The next thing on my list was a trip to the firework tent. I drove an extra ten miles out of town, past three of those pop-up tent stores, to make sure no one would see me buying fireworks. For extra precaution, I wore gloves. A man wearing a 'Merica is great shirt had some nerve to ask me about my gloves and if I was planning on planting the fireworks. The tart by his side cackled like he was Jerry Seinfeld doing stand-up. I said I didn't want to get gunpowder on my fragile skin, which shut him up. One of the benefits of being elderly is that people will believe anything you say, and they feel guilty when they think of their grandparents being dead and all.

I read every package. I needed one with a long fuse to have plenty of time to walk away before the first spark lit anything on fire. And the more sparks, the better. Finally, I found the perfect one. The fuse was long and the package guaranteed at least a minute of sparkle.

I set it on the cashier's table, and he stared at me like I'd just fallen off the turnip truck. He told me my celebration would be pretty short with only one firework. Crap. I hadn't thought to buy more, and I could've kicked myself. The first thing that came to my mind popped out of my mouth. I told him it was for my son's birthday cake and how the whole country celebrates a baby born on the Fourth of July. He had the nerve to laugh and say he hoped I liked confetti cake. A couple of jerks standing behind me in line laughed too—disrespectful low lives.

On my way home, I replayed all of my mistakes in my mind. I know where I screwed up. I should have been paying attention to how many fireworks everyone bought and got the same amount, even though it would have been a waste. Oh well. One of my superpowers is being average. I might as well be invisible. Anyway, the firework tent doesn't have cameras. There would be no tape for the police to scour looking for the strange customer buying one firework for a birthday cake.

When I got home, I hid the firework behind some boxes in the back of the garage. I left my gloves on to maneuver the case of water into the wheelbarrow. After I made sure none of my busy body neighbors were spying on me, I wheeled the old clunker into the garage and parked it by the back door. That would have to do.

I got one bottle free from the plastic wrap. You would have thought I bought genuine crystals, not crystal clear spring water, the way they had it all wrapped up. I needed to practice squirting the water to see how far I could get it. I wanted to be as far away as possible because I didn't want to get caught on one of those doorbell cameras. Had to refill it from the tap a couple of times before being confident I could get the distance I needed. The bottle got softer with each try and required less force to get it to spray across the yard.

The old can of lighter fluid was on the back of one of the shelves behind the oil. In the backyard, I carefully filled the water bottle to the top with lighter fluid. Got lucky there was enough. A good plan always comes together in the end.

I put the empty can of lighter fluid back on the shelf. I'd wait a couple of weeks before throwing it out. Wish I could write myself a reminder note, but I'm not stupid. Never create evidence. And don't you worry about some nosey person reading this journal because I found the perfect hiding spot thanks to my sweet fur baby using her claws to split a seam on one of the sofa cushions. No search warrant surprises for me.

The only thing left on my list is to wait for those morons to watch the ear-splitting firework show tomorrow.

24

Martha

With Walter patrolling the neighborhood parties and fireworks later this evening, the house is all mine again. I never thought of myself as particularly lucky, but I have to say I've been pretty lucky lately.

I decided to take care of the chores around the house first so I could relax later. While sweeping the front porch, I see the temperature isn't the only thing heating up. I'm glad Walter is keeping an eye on the neighborhood parties. I wipe the sweat from my forehead; time to quit for the day.

After a cool shower, I pour myself some iced tea and put my feet up. I'm ready to crack open the summer must-read, according to everyone. A whodunnit is my favorite, even though I always solve the mystery way before the end.

I find myself reading the same line repeatedly with all the hooting and hollering going on outside. The book will have to wait. Maybe the TV will drown out the noise from the party-goers. Now is the perfect time to indulge in my guilty pleasure. What could be better than popcorn for dinner and stupid TV? This is the life.

During the second episode, my phone chimes with a text from Bonnie.

Happy 4th of July. What are you doing to celebrate?

I smile and text back.

Happy 4th of July to you too. What I'm doing is kind of embarrassing.

Now you have to tell me.

I'm watching Destination Dating.

How funny, me too! Kimber is crazy. Trevor is visiting his mom. She gets nervous when there are fireworks. Last year she called the police and said someone was shooting at her. LOL

I smile. We even like the same TV shows. We continue to text back and forth about the show. It's been longer than I like to admit since I've had a friend. I text Bonnie as the sun is setting.

Are you going to watch the fireworks?

I might go for a walk or be lazy and read my book. I am not up for the crowds today. What about you?

Same. I'm enjoying the quiet house.

25

Walter

Keeping an eye on the neighborhood is easier with the community officer's golf cart. For the most part, everyone is behaving and having a good time.

I snagged a six-pack of beer from some middle school kids. It reminded me of the old days at the mall. As I poured out the opened cans, they squirmed nervously, wondering if I was going to turn them over to the police or, worse, their parents. I let them go with a stern warning that next time I wouldn't be as lenient. I put the cans in the back of my cart. I'll recycle the empties and keep the unopened ones—payment for my hard work.

One of the neighbors offers me a hot dog and a beer. I accept the hot dog but stick with my water bottle. I need to stay alert in case the crowds become rowdy.

I drive by my house to peek in on Martha, and she's watching one of those dating shows she pretends to hate. She's staring at her phone, probably waiting for one of the boys to text her back. I've been so busy lately. She must miss me. I'll make a point to spend some time with her tomorrow.

Before long, the sun starts to set. Everyone makes their way to the golf course for the big show. Frank calls my cell phone to make sure everything is running smoothly. I don't mention the kids drinking. What he doesn't know won't hurt him, plus I already handled the situation. I drive the cart up and down the course path to ensure things continue running smoothly. Poor little Grace got burnt on a sparkler. Luckily I had burn cream and an ice pack in my first aid kit. She was back to smiling in no time.

When the show begins, I park the golf cart along a row of pine trees just off the path and put my feet up. The only sounds other than the boom of the fireworks are the oohs and ahhs from the crowd. It's been another successful Fourth of July, thanks to me.

26

Journal

My therapist once told me to focus on what I can control and to let go of what I can't. I could not prevent the neighbors from putting up those awful signs. However, I can control how they will come down.

My plan swirled in my head as the little park in the center of the neighborhood filled with people, ready to barbeque before the firework show. They sat in their lawn chairs, drinking and smoking, not paying any attention to their screaming kids.

With all the hatred in the world, it's remarkable that there are still people like me willing to take action and stand up for what's right. I was as excited as a possum eating sweet taters when the lazy good-for-nothings moseyed to the golf course for the fireworks.

When the coast was clear, I slid on the sweatshirt and pulled the hood over my head. I carefully placed the firework in the front pouch.

Gripping the water bottle in my gloved hand, I headed toward the alley through my neighbor's back yards. About three houses down, I remembered I didn't have the lighter. I had no choice but to hurry back to get it. I wished I had made sure the lighter worked earlier because there was no way I wanted to try it now. I'd burst into flames if I had lighter fluid on my gloves. I decided that if the lighter didn't work when I got to those distasteful signs, the good Lord was taking control, telling me this was a bad plan. Sneaking back down the alley, I heard the familiar booms of the fireworks.

I arrived at the offensive signs and popped open the water bottle's lid, quickly squirting the lighter fluid on as many of them as possible. I hit at least five. With the rest, I aimed for that vile flag.

I needed to ditch the water bottle before I lit up those signs. No way was I taking a chance and ending up in the hospital, all burnt up. The jig would be up for sure.

A couple of houses down, I spotted one of those recycle bins sitting at the curb. Thank you for making my life easier tree-hugging neighbors. Even if some moron spotted me from their dumb doorbell camera, they would think I'm a tree hugger doing right by the earth.

After ditching the bottle, I moseyed back and slipped the glove into my back pocket because I still couldn't get the image of me going up in flames out of my head. I flicked the lighter and thanked the infant baby Jesus when it lit right up. The fuse on the firework caught fire and I threw it right at the signs, praying it was the last time I ever had to see them again. I heard the whoosh as I walked away. I dipped down the alley and hurried to my back yard, where I shoved the sweatshirt into the bottom of a stack of old planters leaned against my little garden shed's back wall. Don't you worry. I remembered to rinse my gloves with dish soap and hot water in the kitchen before returning them to the shed.

The sirens of the fire trucks followed the booms of the grand finale. I did it. The neighborhood is a peaceful place again, thanks to me.

27

Walter

My nose detects the smoke before I hear the sirens. The house's lawn at our neighborhood's entrance is in flames. The fire has already reached the garage, where a pile of lumber sits waiting for a home improvement project. The dry wood fuels the fire, and the fire jumps to the back of the pickup truck in the driveway. Red-hot flames grab hold of the mud flaps and dance around the tires.

A firefighter uses an axe to break down the front door yelling, "Fire! Anyone home?" Four more firefighters enter and return minutes later, declaring the house is secure.

The unlucky family runs down the street. I grab Mrs. Shelby to stop her before she gets too close.

"My home!" she screams.

Mr. Shelby runs for the house, but a firefighter stops him and forces him to turn back. Their two teenage boys stare at the fire from the back of the crowd. A fireman asks the couple if there are any humans or animals in the home.

"No one is in the house. We were at the fireworks. How could this happen?" Mrs. Shelby asks, her voice racked with sobs.

"The investigator will come by in the morning when they can inspect the area in the daylight," the firefighter assures her. "If I had to guess, I would say it could have been a rogue firework or someone tossing a cigarette. With not much rain, this whole area is a tinderbox."

"I can't believe this happened. Everything was fine when we left for the fireworks," Mrs. Shelby cries as her husband puts a protective arm around her shoulder.

"At least everyone is safe," I try to reassure her. "Can I do anything for you? I can run home and grab you some water or a blanket."

"We are fine. Thank you," Mrs. Shelby says, burying her head in her husband's chest.

I direct the crowd to go home so the firefighters can do their job. The couple sits in their neighbor's lawn chairs with blank stares as the firefighters work to contain the fire. I keep an eye on their teenage boys. They are acting suspiciously. After a while, they reluctantly head over and plop down on the ground next to their parents.

"Nothing to see here," I repeat, encouraging the neighbors to disperse.

In less than half an hour, the fire is entirely out. A firefighter does a final spray to ensure no hot spots remain.

Time for me to head home too, but I better return the golf cart to Frank first. On my way, I stop at a recycle bin to throw in the empty beer cans I confiscated from those hooligans. The last thing I need is for Frank to think I was drinking on the job. The faint scent of lighter fluid greets my nose when I lift the lid. A plastic water bottle sits on top of the cardboard boxes that fill the bin. Using the napkin from the hot dog I ate earlier, I carefully pick up the bottle and sniff the top—undeniably lighter fluid.

I walk to one of the firefighters to inform him of my finding, "Sorry to bother you. I am a community officer," I tell him, pointing to the badge on my chest. "I was putting some beer cans in the recycle bin and detected the scent of lighter fluid." The young man raises his eyebrow.

I clear my throat before clarifying, "I confiscated them from underage teens earlier tonight. However, when I smelled the lighter fluid, I did a little digging and found this water bottle to be the culprit. Do you think it's linked to the fire?" I ask, handing him the bottle.

He asks me to clarify which bin as he puts the bottle in a plastic bag marked "evidence." After thanking me for my help, he rolls the recycle bin into the driveway and drapes it in yellow tape.

Before dropping the golf cart at Frank's house, I swing by my house to put the unopened beers on the porch. A glance in the window reveals Martha is sleeping on the sofa. She's so sweet and peaceful, even covered in popcorn. I can't wait to tell her about my exceptional sleuthing skills.

28

Martha

A sea of popcorn surrounds me when I'm startled by keys rattling in the door. Darn it; I fell asleep holding my popcorn bowl. I shoo the cat away from his unexpected feast and scoop like crazy to grab as much as possible, shoving it back into the bowl. Walter bounds into the room, talking a mile a minute.

"Slow down. You're going to have a heart attack," I say, brushing popcorn remnants on the floor. Hopefully, he won't notice that I broke the "no eating in the living room" policy again. But let's face it; the rule only applies to Walter since I do all the cleaning.

Energy radiates from his body as he tells me about his day. Unable to contain his excitement, he paces the floor, filling me in on every detail. The preteens drinking, little Grace getting burned, and how he found some evidence concerning a fire.

"I heard one of the neighbors say they will post on the neighborhood Facebook page for footage from doorbell cameras in the area to check for any suspicious behavior. I wish we still had one of those. It would be an awesome tool to solve the crimes right in our own front yard."

Walter installed a doorbell camera about a year ago, but it made me jump a mile every time my phone alerted me to a movement on the porch. Most of the time, it was only the Amazon delivery person. Those packages are supposed to bring joy, not cardiac arrest. After I yelled at a girl scout to get off the porch or I would call the police, I knew it was time for the camera to go. In my defense, she was pretty old to be a girl scout, and it did appear like she was trying to open my door to rob me and not drop off my cookies.

Walter is still talking, "The fire inspector will be there tomorrow. I thought I should be there to help with the investigation. Since I was on the lookout all day, I'm sure I can answer questions about what everyone was up to."

"That is a splendid idea. You can help crack the case," I encourage.

"Who knew being a community officer would be so important?" he says, finally sitting next to me on the sofa.

"You have always been important to me," I assure him with a smile.

"You won't be too lonely with me gone?" he asks, taking my hand and giving it a little squeeze.

"Don't worry about me. Keeping our community safe is important," I reassure him. "I can find something to do while you're busy."

29

Journal

That no-good therapist used to tell me to see if my intentions matched the outcome. I wonder if she intended to leave me to figure out how to solve all my problems all by my lonesome.

We all know I intended to beautify the entrance to my neighborhood by removing that hideous flag and obnoxious signs, so hold your horses on the judging about the fire spreading. That wasn't my intention, but I give credit where credit is due. That was all the good Lord's doing. The hand of God Almighty came down and removed that filth from the face of the earth. I only provided the means to do his handiwork.

The word on the community Facebook page is they found my water bottle, and the police are searching for doorbell camera footage. Part of living in a small community is that nosey neighbors are always in your business. I'm not worried. I took all those steps for a reason. The hours spent watching crime shows will save me from an arson charge. Time well spent if you ask me.

The neighborhood was out lollygagging when I went by the house this morning. I tried not to smile but was happy as a pig in slop. All those shameless signs were ash on the ground along with that horrific flag. You're welcome.

30

Walter

I'm laying on a stack of Martha's famous french toast heaped high with fresh strawberries and dripping in my favorite maple syrup from the farmer's market. The fire chief hands me a medal of honor while Frank looks on with his hands shoved deep in his pockets. My eyes pop open right before I start my speech, but it doesn't matter because I'm positive my dream will come true. There wouldn't be any evidence if it weren't for me.

As I walk down the stairs, the first thing that greets me is the scent of cinnamon. When I waltz into the kitchen, Martha flips a piece of french toast on the griddle. My dream is already coming true.

"A hero deserves a hero's breakfast." She smiles and pours me a steaming cup of coffee.

"I'm not a hero," I say modestly, taking a seat at the table. *This is going to be a wonderful day.*

"You spent your holiday helping our community. That is a hero in my book." She kisses the top of my balding head.

The french toast melts in my mouth, and I am again thankful

for Martha's cooking. I am a lucky man. She works hard to keep me well-fed and our little house tidy.

Even though we haven't kept up with the Joneses, our house is charming and comfortable. The linoleum on the kitchen floor is a little worse for wear. However, every one of those stains and cracks reminds me of when our family filled this room with laughter. The boys and their friends crowded around the table for pizza and ice cream on Saturday night. And my sweet Martha made Sunday morning breakfast with all the fixings before church. She has always made our house a home.

Martha leaves me to finish my breakfast so she can start her chores. While she's busy cleaning the guest bathroom no one ever uses, I take the opportunity to grab some money out of the secret desk drawer. Martha works so hard around here I decide to ask if I should pick up something to grill for dinner. I'm sure she would appreciate a night off from cooking.

She yells out the bathroom door, "That sounds lovely. How much money is left? I would love to ask Bonnie for coffee."

I quickly grab another twenty. "No need to worry, dear. I'll leave some money on the counter for you."

I'm out the door before she comes out of the bathroom. I don't need more questions.

I walk the short distance to the crime scene, and twenty neighbors are already gawking at the damage. It takes me a minute to spot the inspector. Is he even out of the academy? I bet he is younger than the shoes on my feet. His shirt is too tight, wrinkled, and light pink. His wife must have washed it with something red. No professional officer would wear a pink shirt. He doesn't even have it tucked in all the way, and his tie is too loose for my liking. It's like he just crawled out of bed.

I walk over to introduce myself. "Good morning. I'm Walter," I say, sticking my hand out for him to shake. "I was the community officer on duty last night. How can I help?"

He half-heartedly shakes my hand and replies, "You are the man I was looking for. Can you come to the police station to answer some questions about the activities around the neighborhood last night?"

"I would be happy to. Unfortunately, my wife has the car today. Can it wait until later this afternoon or tomorrow?"

"I can give you a lift," he suggests. "Just need to finish up here."

"Sounds good," I agree.

I stand to the side to observe. He searches the shrubs like it's an Easter egg hunt. Next, he moves to the back of the house. The fire was in the front, you idiot. He talks to a few neighbors and writes in a tiny notebook, like the ones Martha used to put in the boy's stockings. Is this guy serious?

More than sixty minutes pass before he asks if I'm ready to go. My hip is throbbing from standing around. No one bothered to offer me a chair. No respect nowadays for the people who serve the community. These new officers are terrible. They certainly don't respect anyone's time. When you are young, you have all the time in the world. When you're old, you need to take advantage of every minute you have left.

The ride to the police station does not improve the situation. I take in the view like I am trying to commit the outside world to my memory. Why do I feel like I'm going to jail? I helped find the crucial piece of evidence to crack the case. This town would be lost without me. The ride is only made worse by the small talk the officer is trying to engage me in. Maybe if he had shown me more respect and not wasted my time, I would have given him advice on how to have a great life and successful career like I did. This young whippersnapper doesn't deserve my wisdom. I am relieved when we finally arrive at the station.

The lead detective greets me with a firm handshake. "Come on back. I have a couple of questions for you, sir."

I am glad he is prompt and shows me the respect I deserve. He leads me back to a door marked INTERVIEW ROOM and holds the door open, allowing me to enter first. A rectangular metal table and two matching metal chairs, chained to the floor, sit in the room. A small television in a plastic box is attached to the wall near the ceiling. The door thuds closed behind him. My mouth goes dry. The detective pulls out one of the chairs, and I wince at the screech of metal against the floor. He waves me to the seat across from him and sets a voice recorder on the table.

"Thank you for coming down to the station. We like to interview witnesses as soon as possible so facts won't become muddled with rumors or forgotten altogether. The lab detected an accelerant in the water bottle you found. We were also able to lift a fingerprint and discovered it belonged to you. The fireman said you handed him the bottle using a napkin. Any idea how your fingerprints got on the bottle?"

My mind starts racing a mile a minute. I can feel the sweat forming on my forehead. He can't possibly think I have something to do with this. Can he?

"My only guess is that I accidentally touched it. I had never seen it before I opened the recycle bin to put in the empty cans I confiscated from the underage kids." I feel the flush creep over my cheeks. "I wanted to put them in a recycle bin to dispose of them properly, and it was pure luck when I opened the bin and smelled the lighter fluid. That particular smell reminds me of camping with my kids. I swear I was at the golf course watching the fireworks with everyone else." My mouth is so dry my throat clicks when I try to swallow. A bead of sweat drips down my forehead, making me appear guilty as hell.

"Hold up and slow down. I'll grab you some water," the detective says and leaves the room.

He returns holding a bottle of water similar to the one I found. Is this a trick? He waits for me to take a drink before he continues, "We are aware of your location when the fire started. Five witnesses confirmed you were watching the fireworks in a golf cart at the course. Grace's mother told us how you came to the rescue with the burn cream right before the fireworks started, and according to the footage on a doorbell camera in the area, the fire started during that time frame."

"Okay," I say, wiping the persistent sweat from my forehead with the back of my hand.

"We're hoping you might recognize the person the doorbell camera captured lurking around," he says and nods toward the mirror behind me.

The screen on the tiny television comes to life. The picture is grainy and dark, and the suspect never turns in the camera's direction. No one would be able to identify anything from the footage.

"Looks like a teenage boy," I say, squinting at the screen. "The homeowners have two teenage boys who seemed suspicious. Did you question them?"

"Not yet. They are on my list. What do you mean by suspicious?"

He leans on the table, making a steeple with his fingers, and stares at me.

I clear my throat, "They were whispering, and they hung back from the scene for quite some time before they joined their parents."

"Did they say anything to make you think they were somehow involved?" he asks, sitting back in his chair.

"No, as I said, they were whispering." I have no idea why he is making me nervous. I was born to be a good witness with my attention to detail and spot-on intuition.

He pushes back from the table, making his chair screech across the floor again. "Okay, thank you, sir. That's all for today. Would you like an officer to give you a ride home?"

I politely decline. Rumors would fly through the entire neighborhood. No, thank you.

31

Martha

I text Bonnie to ask if she's free to grab a coffee this morning. She texts back immediately. "YES" with three exclamation points and a smiley face emoji. My smile is as big as the emoji.

As I leave the neighborhood, I spot Walter talking to a young man in a pretty pink shirt in front of the burned-up yard.

Bonnie is sitting in a bright blue Adirondack chair on the front porch of the local coffee shop, Beans And Greens. She wears a flowing sundress and a wide-brimmed hat, making her look fancy and relaxed at the same time. She is average in weight and height yet way above average in style. Her wavy hair flows down her back from under her hat. Her perfect makeup and jewelry make her appear more put together than I have ever been. Once we are more acquainted, I will ask where she shops so I can copy her style, but only a little.

When Bonnie spots me, she waves me over and leads me through the quaint shop to a spot on the outdoor deck. This area is lovely, with small bistro tables and chairs in all different colors with little vases of fresh-cut flowers in the center of every table. The view of the mountains in the distance is breathtaking, and it reminds me how thankful I am to live in such a beautiful place. We order our drinks and decide to split a zucchini muffin that is bigger than my head.

"I am so glad you texted. Cleaning the bathroom was on the agenda for this morning, but this is ten million times better!" Bonnie says before taking a sip of her chai tea.

"I should be home doing the same thing, but I'm bored doing the same chores in the same house. Maybe next week we should trade housework," I half joke.

"You should at least check out my house before you offer that deal. My Trevor can make quite the mess, and he somehow forgot how to clean as soon as I quit working outside the home," Bonnie says, rolling her eyes and laughing. "Did you hear the fire trucks last night?" she asks, changing the subject.

"I fell asleep on the couch and missed all the excitement. It was quite the scene this morning."

"You must sleep like a rock. It was so loud I thought the whole neighborhood was ablaze. I admit I was pretty happy those terrible signs were destroyed." She grins like the Cheshire Cat.

"Me too, and I am glad no one was hurt. Walter is helping with the investigation." I roll my eyes despite myself.

"I hope he figures out what happened so I can chip in for the culprit's legal defense." Bonnie winks.

The conversation flows smoothly into predictions about what will happen next on *Destination Dating*.

"How is your daughter doing?" I ask, getting around to more important talk.

"There are days when I think she will be okay because Dave

seems to be treating her better. But most days, I'm worried about what the next phone call will bring," Bonnie sighs. "I worry about what Trevor might do to fix the situation. He got so angry when he saw a bruise on Ashley's face that he confronted the scumbag. Trevor told Dave if he ever laid a hand on his daughter or grandson again, God would have to help him because his life would be over before the police had time to show up. I thought the threat was working until I discovered Dave is being more careful to put the bruises in less prominent places, and we aren't welcome at the house anymore."

"I am so sorry you have to go through this. It's hard when a family member is struggling, and you feel powerless," I tell her, trying to be encouraging.

Bonnie takes a bite from the muffin and shakes her head in agreement.

"When I was in high school, my daddy was diagnosed with leukemia," I share, hoping to sound relatable. "We knew the chemical plant where he had worked for twenty years was to blame. Fifty people worked in his department, and thirteen had leukemia."

"How terrible! Did you sue them?" Bonnie asks, her eyes wide.

"Our lawyer recommended a class-action lawsuit because they are usually the most cost-effective option. But the plant hired a team of lawyers. Their expert witnesses said it was a coincidence that they all got the same illness simultaneously. They filed motion after motion delaying the court case and costing the families thousands of dollars."

"I've heard of lawyers doing that," Bonnie sighs. "The cases get stuck in court, so most people can't afford to keep spending money. What did you do?"

"I got so angry by the injustice of it all and that nothing would change the fact that my daddy was sick. I lost myself to the anger and yelled at anyone who would listen. I even quit going to church for a while. I couldn't believe God would let my daddy suffer while those people got away with murder. When I showed up at the company owner's office, the cops arrested me for refusing to leave. No one cared. My daddy was dying because of what they did to him, and those people couldn't be bothered to talk to me. Shortly after that, the panic attacks started. I don't usually tell anyone this, but they got so bad I spent a few days at the local hospital's psych ward."

"That sounds scary," Bonnie says, gently putting her hand on mine. "What happened next?"

"I decided to pick myself up because I needed to be strong for my parents, and the good book says *God doesn't give us more than we can handle.* After over a year of fighting in the courts, the other families had had enough and wanted to settle. I wanted to keep fighting, but I couldn't do it alone. I wasn't sleeping or eating and knew if I kept going like that, I would've ended up right back in the hospital. We had to put Daddy in a nursing home because my mama couldn't handle his medical needs. We knew he wouldn't live to enjoy any money we would win in the lawsuit anyway, so we gave up. The company settled, and each family walked away with fifty-thousand dollars. We paid the attorney and the rest went to Daddy's care.

"To make matters worse, a few months after Daddy passed, my mama went to bed and never woke up. The doctor said she died of a heart attack, but I knew it was a broken heart. The only thing I wanted was to get out of there. Mississippi held too many horrible memories. The day after Mama's funeral, I loaded up my car, stopped by the cemetery to tell my parents goodbye, and drove away. I've never looked back."

"I am so sorry. That sounds like it was so hard," Bonnie says gently. "How did you pick up the pieces?"

"Well, I knew I couldn't drive around forever, even though it sounded like a great plan at the time. Thankfully days later, when I drove into North Carolina, I felt I was home. I got a job at the orthodontist's office in the billing department. Walter came in for a mouthguard because he was grinding his teeth. He flirted with me after his appointment. Said I was too pretty to work in the back of the office. Later he sent me a dozen roses with the check to pay his bill. He had written the cutest poem on the card. I'll never forget it,

'Roses are red
Martha is sweet
If she will go out to dinner with me
My life will be complete.'

He wasn't exactly a poet, but he was what I needed. A good, hardworking man who loved me."

Bonnie smiles. "What a sweet story."

"Your turn. How did you meet Trevor?" I ask.

"We met at a bar. Ours is a typical love story: girl gets drunk, sleeps with man, finds herself pregnant, decides what the hell, let's start a family together." Bonnie laughs. "We've had some rocky patches, but for the most part, we are happy. Isn't it crazy how life works? If I had gone into a different bar that night, my whole life would be different." Bonnie gazes into the distance.

My phone buzzes. Walter needs a ride home from the police station. Why did I talk so much? I promise Bonnie that she can do all the talking at our next painting class. I hope I haven't ruined my chance at a true friendship. It feels so nice to have someone to talk to.

"Hope the police didn't charge Walter with last night's

neighborhood beautification," Bonnie says. "I am happy to chip in for his defense."

"I'm sure he was only helping with the investigation or joining another task force," I sigh.

"I'm so excited about painting on Tuesday," she calls after me as I head for the car.

32

Walter

When I see Martha pull up to the entrance of the police station, I hurry to the car. "Thank you for picking me up," I say, slumping in the passenger seat.

"No problem. What's happening with the investigation? Do they know what started the fire?"

"They suspect teens of foul play."

"If anyone can catch a delinquent, it's you, dear. Should we stop at the store?" Martha suggests.

"Not now. I need to call Frank to tell him about the investigation. The image of the potential perpetrator is still fresh in my mind, and I want to help before it fades. I'll stop by the store later."

"Okay. Do you want me to go with you, or should I make a list? If you keep buying all my fancy favorites, we'll end up in the poor house." She glances at me and reaches for my hand.

"Don't you worry, dear. We could never be poor when we are so rich in love," I reassure her with a smile and take her hand in mine.

Later I will also be rich in cash when I hand in my winning scratcher and buy a few more.

I call Frank as soon as I walk in the door. "Hi Frank, it's Walter," I yell into the phone for Frank's benefit.

"Hi, Wally," he shouts.

I brush off his lack of respect to inform him of my valuable assistance with the case.

"The other community officers and I have been going door-to-door to ask if anyone has camera footage from last night," Frank yells. I have to hold the phone away from my ear to avoid a broken ear drum. "I picked up some *Neighborhood Watch* and *Community Committed to Peace* signs to distribute around the neighborhood. Everyone needs to know that acts of violence will not be tolerated around here. If you swing by, I'll give you a map of the area you can canvas."

I tell him I'll be over soon and hang up. Martha is staring at me. Her eyes are sad.

"Want to come along?" I ask, hoping she says no.

"No, that's okay. I have my class tomorrow, so I will finish my housework and make a grocery list. I'll leave the crime-fighting to you experts."

Is that a hint of sarcasm in her voice? Nah, my Martha knows I'm a hero.

33

Martha

Maybe it was the extra coffee or the adrenaline rush of making a new friend, but I cleaned the upstairs bathroom, started the laundry, scooped the kitty litter, and whipped up my famous homemade brownies in record time. Walter has no idea I hide pureed spinach in his favorite brownies. While they bake, I sit down to enjoy an episode of *Destination Dating*. Two girls have a hair-pulling fight and get kicked off the island. "So much for your free vacation," I say aloud. I text Bonnie.

Sorry I had to leave in a rush. Guess what I'm doing now?

Hopefully not bailing Walter out of jail!

Ha! No! Thank goodness!

Might you be watching Kimber being kicked off the island with mascara running down her face?

How did you know?

I am doing the same thing! I cleaned for fifteen minutes, though—laughing emoji.

I can't wait to find out who ends up with the stunning dress they keep showing in the ad teasers!

I will be sad when it's over.

Me too! We will have to wait a year for more of our guilty pleasure. The other reality shows don't measure up to DD!

We might have to give Arranged Marriage: Mom Knows Best a try.

Good plan. It might help with the withdrawal.

We text back and forth during every commercial break. As the final credits roll across the screen Bonnie texts.

She was so beautiful in the dress—heart-eye emoji.

Do you think they will make it?

Nope. Never do. Real life has a way of slapping you in the face. Plus, kids nowadays expect everything to be easy. No one wants to work for what they want or believe in. I wish everyone could be perfect like us—smiley face emoji.

The world would be a better place—winky face emoji.

I get busy cleaning up the kitchen and see a whole row of brownies are missing. No more eating while I watch TV, I tell myself while I place the rest of the brownies on a plate and then wash the pan. At least they were healthy. A long walk is in order, and I better add some fruit and veggies to the grocery list. I text Bonnie.

Care to join me on a walk?

Three dots show up, disappear, then show up again. I may have pushed my luck. Finally, a text comes through.

I would love that. Getting my shoes on and heading your way. We can meet in the middle.

My cheeks lift in a big smile. I rush to put my sneakers on and then scribble a quick note for Walter so he won't worry.

Bonnie and I meet at the park in the middle of the neighborhood. We chat effortlessly as Bonnie spills the tea on all the neighbors. When we walk by the house at the entrance to the neighborhood, she comments on how lovely the new welcome sign is, and I agree. Almost anything would be better than the political signs that used to welcome people to our little neighborhood. A pile of trash sits by the curb with the melted mud flaps on top.

"She's not so perky now, is she?" Bonnie asks, pointing to the melted rubber woman.

I burst out laughing. A neighbor turns to glare at us, and I slap my hand over my mouth. We pivot and walk back the way we came. After one more loop around the neighborhood, Bonnie says she should be getting back to finish her chores. She hugs me, and I practically dance home. It is so lovely to have a friend to walk and laugh with.

34

Walter

Going door to door is exhilarating. I carry a properly sized notebook to take precise notes. You never know what you might learn if you pay close enough attention. A dark hoodie hangs on a hook in the home of a teen who is usually up to no good. I add the valuable observation to my notebook.

Two neighbors share footage from their doorbell cameras. The cameras are too far from the crime scene. Nonetheless, the footage could contain evidence. I strategically put the *Neighborhood Watch* and the *Community Committed to Peace* signs throughout the neighborhood. They welcome everyone into our little section of town, show we care about each other, and actively create a safe environment.

By the time I finish interrogating the neighbors and placing the last sign, it is already three-thirty. I hurry home to check on Martha, but she isn't home. Her note says that she and Bonnie went for a walk. A plate of brownies is on the counter—my stomach growls. I forgot to eat lunch. I grab a brownie off the plate and eat it as I drive to the senior center.

Some old guys sit around a table playing cards. One yells over to ask if I want to join them. I scan the table to see if they are betting actual money. When I see a lack of cash or poker chips, I decline and head for the donuts. Four boxes are stacked on the table. The top three are empty. However, the last box has one nutty bar left—score. My next stop will be the lotto counter to continue my luck.

"Well, hi there, sugar," Fran greets me warmly. Her smile brightens up the entire store.

"Hello, how is my lucky charm doing today?" I ask, returning a smile.

"I am doing quite well. What can I do for you?"

"I have a twenty-dollar winner." I slide the card across the counter.

"Oh great! Would you like the cash today?"

"I will go with twelve five-dollar tickets, please. You pick." I pull two twenties out of my wallet and hand them to her.

She chooses my tickets. When she hands them to me, her fingers gently touch mine.

"Wishing you luck, hon."

I go over to the tiny tables set up by the salad bar and start scratching. The first is a five-dollar winner. I'm not ahead yet, but at least I'm breaking even. The following two reveal nothing. But the fourth is a one hundred dollar winner.

Oh! My god!

My chest tingles with excitement as I double-check to ensure my eyes aren't deceiving me. Yup—a one hundred dollar winner!

I scratch the remaining eight cards—all losers. No worries, I think to myself as I saunter back to Fran.

"How did you do?" she asks.

"One hundred and five dollars in winnings!" I say a bit too

loudly, handing her the tickets.

"I am so happy for you. I love when good things happen to good people. How would you like your cash? Maybe five twenties and a five-dollar bill?" she suggests.

"How about three twenty-dollar tickets and the rest in cash."

She hands me three "Living Large" tickets and forty-five dollars in cash. The cards are enormous. I have to fold them in half to shove them into my back pocket. I'll continue my lucky streak later but now I need to find something for dinner.

The young woman behind the meat counter suggests the chuck eye steak because they are running a sale. I am a sucker for a good deal, so chuck eye steaks it is.

35

Fran

The lotto counter has been steady all day, and I struggle to maintain a positive attitude. Between all the people already wearing shirts for that good-for-nothing candidate in the upcoming election and every customer appearing to be more desperate than the last, I'm depressed.

I feel like a dealer selling my clients their drug of choice. They can't stop using it, and I need to make the sale to keep my job. I am always hopeful that once they are ahead, even a little, they will quit. That never happens. Even my subtle hint of asking how they want their cash doesn't make them rethink their choices and take the damn money.

"Do you think you can get your hands on some more of those *Gamblers Anonymous* fliers?" I ask Susan when I walk into her office for my break, shutting the door behind me.

"Probably. Do you think we need them?" She doesn't look up from the stack of paperwork in front of her.

"Yes, I do. It makes me sad to see all the older people on fixed incomes wasting their money. I always try to be extra friendly, so at least they are getting something out of all that cash they waste."

Susan sets her pen on the pile of papers and walks around her desk to give me a hug.

"You are an amazing woman with a big heart. I am lucky to have you," she whispers in my ear before pulling away to look me in my eyes. "I promise to order more fliers ASAP."

"Thank you my love." I smile at her sweetly.

Susan grins and adds, "Did you ever think that your charm makes those old fellas want to buy all those tickets?"

"No way! They know I am just doing my job," I insist, planting my hands on my hips. "And as long as you're ordering signs, how about getting some *Hate Has No Home Here* signs for the store? I was happy to see those terrible political signs replaced with those at the entrance to our neighborhood."

"I promise to get a hold of the store owner and check," she says, glancing at her watch. "Oh shoot! How is it after four o'clock already? I need to make sure the delivery truck arrived. You finish your break in here for some peace and quiet," she tells me, heading for the door.

"We should also fly a rainbow flag out front while we're at it. A small one for the lotto counter would be a great addition."

"I don't think so, darling. Lotto sales will plummet if those old fellas don't think you're available. Plus it is so much fun to have a secret." Susan winks at me as she walks out the door, closing it behind her.

36

Journal

I'm tickled pink. You will never believe this. I went for a stroll to check on my little neck of the woods. At the entrance, the awful signs I burned down had been replaced with ones promoting the neighborhood watch organization and others welcoming folks to our peaceful community. My favorite said, "Hate Has No Home Here." Well, butter my butt and call me a biscuit. I changed our neighborhood overnight.

My mama always said that even a tiny spark of love would chase out the darkness of hatred, and by golly, she was right.

37

Walter

After a delicious dinner, I sneak into the bathroom to continue my lucky streak. Martha's tweezers easily remove the silver coating on my lotto cards.

The first one is defective. Damn it. So is the second, but I have a good feeling about the last one. The goal is to spell Lucky with the letters hidden under the silver coating. I have an L, U, K, and Y with two more bubbles to scratch. The first is an M, not even close. The last had a round front like a C, but as I scratched further, it turned out to be an O.

I plop down on the toilet, put my head between my knees, and take a few deep breaths. It feels like someone punched me in the gut. Sixty dollars down the drain in less than ten minutes.

"Think, think, think," I whisper.

I need to get rid of the evidence. I wipe off the tweezers with a tissue and place them in the exact spot I found them. Next, I tear one of the tickets into little pieces, wrap them in toilet paper, throw the wad into the bowl, and hit the flusher. I repeat the process with the remaining tickets.

Martha might wonder why I've been in here for so long. The best way to handle this situation is with the lilac-scented spray she insists I use when nature calls. I spray a heavy dose and then set the bottle on the back of the toilet. Are you kidding me? Part of a ticket floats in the water. The $20 in bold print mocks me. I hit the flusher again, and watch the tiny piece swirl around the bowl and appear to disappear. However, a second later, it is floating in the water again. No, no, no. I grab a piece of toilet paper and fish it out—the lengths I have to go to cover my tracks. I tear the tiny piece into even smaller pieces, turn on the sink faucet and watch as they swirl down the drain. While I wash my hands, I stare into the sink, expecting them to reappear. They don't. Thank God.

Glancing at my face in the mirror, I look older than my years. When did my hair become so thin? Oh well, I can't stay young forever.

Martha is glued to the television when I return to the living room.

"Are you okay, dear?" she asks, not taking her eyes off the TV.

"Just a little tummy trouble. I'm going to go to bed."

"Let me know if I can get you anything. Maybe tea or some Pepto Bismol."

"Thank you, dear. I'll be okay."

I trudge up the stairs to the bedroom. At least I didn't lie to Martha about being sick to my stomach.

38

Walter

My mood is slightly better after a good night's rest. I drop Martha off at the community center for her self-defense class and then hightail it to the ReStore. I have three hours to get this project finished. The last thing I need is for Martha to realize the fence panels aren't brand new. What she doesn't know won't hurt her. A man with my skills can have the recycled panels looking good as new in no time.

I walk as fast as my lousy hip allows through the store, past the used furniture, paint, and various nuts and bolts to the very back. Once there, I find six panels in decent shape marked twenty dollars each. I like this price much better than the fifty-five apiece they want at the hardware store. I head to the front of the store to the perky clerk with purple hair and a face full of hardware.

"Good morning, sugar. How can I help you today?" she asks, smacking on a large wad of pink bubble gum.

"I would like the six fence panels in the back, and I need them delivered today. The sooner, the better," I tell her, reaching for my wallet.

"I can ring those up for you. But we don't have any delivery spots until next week. Would Monday work?" she asks, flipping through an old notebook on the counter while blowing a huge bubble.

"That won't work. I need them right now." My brain races through my contacts. I quickly conclude that I don't know anyone with a truck. The people in line behind me are getting impatient as I urge my brain to find a solution.

"Hey, old timer, I can deliver your panels right now for forty bucks." I turn around to see a young punk covered in tattoos, drooping jeans, and smelling like a skunk high on bad weed.

I despise the term old timer, but I'm out of options.

"Alright," I sigh.

He helps me load the panels into his rusted-out truck. I hand him a twenty and promise the rest of the money upon delivery. When I give him my address, he doesn't write it down or program it into his phone—another red flag. I tell him to follow me. At least that way, I can keep my eyes on him.

He tailgates me as we leave the parking lot, which helps me relax a little. Maybe I shouldn't have judged him based on his appearance. Martha always says, "Don't judge a book by its cover."

Less than a minute later, I glance in my rearview mirror, and he's vanished. I slow down, hoping he will reappear. When I arrive at the entrance to my neighborhood, he is still nowhere in sight. How could I have been so stupid? All that money is down the drain, and I have no fence panels. I'll have to buy all ten panels for full price at the hardware store. Defeated, I head home feeling nauseous and foolish. I need to count the rest of the money and devise a new plan before I pick up Martha.

As I turn the corner to my street, I see the punk's truck in my driveway. He's unloading the panels and leaning them against the house. A wave of relief washes over me.

"Hey there, old timer, what took you so long?" he asks, taking out the last panel.

"Us old people drive slow," I chuckle out of pure relief.

"Apparently. When I passed you, you were going twenty under the speed limit. You gotta be more careful and keep your eyes on the road," he laughs.

Is he lecturing me? I don't even care. I almost hug him when I give him the other twenty.

"Want to earn another twenty and help me put these panels in place?" I ask, fully aware of the increasing cloud cover. The rain is on its way, and I need to finish before the heavens open up.

"Sure, old timer. I can call it my good deed of the day." He slaps me on the back—hard.

We remove the worst of the rotted panels but leave the posts. I'm surprised at how well we work together. He is strong and can carry each one over his head like a superhero. Between his strength and my nail gun expertise we finish in record time.

"I can take these old panels off your hands," he offers.

I weigh my options. I could create one good panel if I took the old ones apart. Although, if I let him take them now, I won't have to pay later to have them hauled away. With my approval, he loads the old panels into his truck.

After power washing all of the panels we installed, I stand back to survey my handiwork. Up close, it's obvious they aren't brand new. But from a distance, they look great. I decide not to worry about it. The chances of Martha examining my work up close are slim to none.

I will purchase the remaining four panels for the side yard while

Martha is at her painting class. I hope that she won't ask why I didn't get them all at the same time. The last thing I want to do is lie to her.

39

Martha

Once again, I am the first person sitting in the circle of chairs in the gym. I sit in the same chair I chose last time. This is the best seat, after all. A grin grows across my face as I ponder how well I'm doing in this class. The door to the gym opens, and Titus saunters over to sit in the chair next to me.

"Good morning, Martha. Did you notice that you were more observant of the people around you since our last class?"

"Good morning, Titus. Now that you mention it, I did make a new friend since our last class. Probably because I was paying more attention to people around me."

"That's marvelous. Like I said last week, being aware of your surroundings can protect you from something dangerous or help you notice wonderful things, like a new friend. Do you think you missed opportunities for new friendships in the past?" Titus asks.

"Honestly, it has been years since I interacted with new people," I admit sheepishly.

"I am glad this class is proving helpful to you, Martha." He stands. "I need to go grab the materials we need for today. I'll be back," he says over his shoulder as he walks to the supply closet.

The other students begin wandering in. Julie plops down next to me, her granddaughter in tow.

"Not sure how I feel about this class," Julie whispers to me out of the side of her mouth. "The instructor is intense."

"I love this class," I say loud enough so everyone can hear.

"I do too," she says, trying to sound like she wasn't bashing the class moments ago.

Titus strides into the room with a loud greeting, "Good morning," his voice echoes off the walls of the large gym. "Today, we will start with a five-minute meditation to help you become more aware of your surroundings. Let's head outside and get started."

When we are all outside, everyone finds a spot to sit for the meditation. Julie leans against a white SUV, which I assume is her car. She looks like she is ready to bolt.

"Take a minute to observe your surroundings," Titus instructs.

I notice several kids playing on a small playground and a couple walking a humongous dog. Several minutes pass, and Titus guides us to close our eyes. He asks us to notice if our surroundings match what we hear.

I hear birds and traffic from the freeway. A bug buzzes by my ear, a child laughs joyfully, and I hear footsteps. I squeeze my eyes shut and cover them with my hands so I won't be tempted to peek.

When the five minutes are finally over, Titus asks if anyone heard anything different from what they saw. Several people say they heard the freeway and kids laughing. I raise my hand, and Titus nods at me.

"I think I heard footsteps right next to me," I report.

"Did anyone else hear footsteps?" Titus asks.

A few of the other students raise their hands.

"Look at the ground next to you, and you will see a lucky penny. While your eyes were closed, I placed a penny near all of you. Some of you could sense my presence because of your heightened awareness. Great job to those of you who did."

I grab my penny and put it in my pocket—a lucky charm to remind me of this moment. Next, we practice our screams. I can't help rolling my eyes as Julie apologizes to strangers in the parking lot. Anyone with any sense can see we are in a class, and no one is being attacked in broad daylight, surrounded by ten people.

As we head back into the building for a water break, Titus says in his drill sergeant voice, "I want everyone to see if you can remember what your second most powerful weapon to use against an attacker is. We will discuss the answer after our water break."

Titus opens the discussion once everyone is sitting in their chairs. I stay silent because I don't want to be a know-it-all.

Julie raises her flabby arm and shouts, "Arms!" She obviously wasn't paying attention.

Her granddaughter sighs and says, "Your legs, Grandma. Even I know that, and I was on my phone most of the class."

"Our high school senior has it," Titus shouts. "A kick has six times the force of a punch. Also, the average person's legs are longer than their arms, so with a kick, you can keep your safety bubble intact and still harm an attacker. We are going to work on a forward push kick."

Titus stands to demonstrate. He places his right leg behind the left, picks his right leg up, kicks forward, and then places it back down.

"As you can see from my demonstration, this is a fast motion.

Because the kick is fast, you don't need to rely on your balance as much. This is important because balance is something most people lose with age. Remember to keep your arms in a fighting stance to protect your face. Can anyone tell me what you should aim for with your kick?"

"The knee," I shout, no longer worried about being a know-it-all. Watching those videos is paying off.

"Yes Martha! A solid kick to the knee can easily take someone out. You can also aim for anywhere on the leg, perhaps the groin, if you are tall or your attacker is short."

We take turns kicking while Titus holds a blocking pad. I am amazed at how much force I create. The pad makes a loud sound each time I kick it, and Titus moves back a little to absorb the energy. Next, we practice a side-kick. My kick is higher, but I feel a bit off balance. Titus lines three mats along the wall, so we can practice using our right and left legs. He instructs us to observe which kick and leg work best for us.

"Great class today, everyone," he says, although he is looking directly at me. "Keep the different kicks in your self-defense toolbox. Put your favorite on the top so it's easily accessible. See you in a week, where you will all get to punch me, and I won't punch back." He grins at his joke.

40

Journal

My incompetent therapist told me to write down what I'm grateful for, and to be mindful of my blessings. I bet she's grateful for all this time off of work, doing absolutely nothing. I have to admit that she may have been on to something though, because after I write my thoughts in this journal, I do feel more blessed.

An evening stroll around my neighborhood was the perfect way to end the day. A person can learn a lot about their neighbors at night when the lights are on, and the blinds are up. And the best part is, my superpower is being invisible. People nowadays don't pay attention with their eyes always on those little phones they carry everywhere.

The night was perfect for a stroll. It was blazing hot during the day, the kind of day where your feet blistered just thinking of walking barefoot on the cement. Then out of nowhere, the heavens opened and unloaded sweet, sweet rain. It was the kind of rain that made everything smell clean. The best part was, it was almost ten degrees cooler when the heavens closed back up. I swear I heard the earth breathe a sigh of relief. As if the sins of all the evildoers were washed clean. Their filthy souls being baptized by holy water from above.

When I rounded the corner to the street beyond mine I couldn't believe my eyes. A young girl dressed like a streetwalker was climbing out a second-story window. Her tank top was so tight I could see the outline of her barely bloomed boobies. The fabric around her waist hardly covered her bottom. I could see straight to the promised land, what a disgrace. Her three-inch heels made the ladder a challenge, but she did it. I would bet she's done this same maneuver before.

She glanced at the front door for a split second and then walked along the neighbor's front hedges before heading to the road. Now, what kind of trouble was she planning to get into? She wobbled to a little red sports car, parked a few houses down, opened the driver's door, and climbed in. My eyes bulged out of my head as I watched her straddle the driver and put her tongue down his throat. Disgusting. She finally got in the passenger seat, not even bothering to buckle up. When they drove past that nasty child gave me a little wink like I was part of the plan all along.

Now, as you know, I don't like to put my nose where it doesn't belong, but I knew for a fact that her mama and daddy didn't have a clue she had skedaddled from her bedroom window dressed like a sex worker. As I got closer to their front door, I could see them sitting on the couch watching a rerun of The Office. Anyone who likes The Office is a decent person in my book, so I decided right then and there I couldn't let those lovely people be made a fool of by their good-for-nothing offspring. I marched right up to the front door and rang the bell.

That girl's daddy whipped open the door and snarled a rude greeting. I had the right mind to turn around and not tell him a thing. Lucky for him, when he looked at me, his tone changed. But then he had the nerve to ask if I was lost. Why do people always think elderly people are stupid or senile?

I told him his ladder was leaning up against his fine home, and I would hate for the wind to catch it and blow it over into his neighbor's window. Of course, he knew nothing about his ladder being out, so I brought him around the side of his house so he could see with his own two eyes. The heavens parted, and he finally knew what was happening. That man was so angry he cussed right in front of me. The hussy's mama heard all the unholy yelling and came out to see what was going on. She saw that ladder and lost it. She started cursing too. He blamed her, and she accused him with words I will not repeat, even in writing. That's when I hightailed it out of there as fast as possible. Their foul language rang in my ears as I made my way down my driveway.

Right place, right time. That's what it boils down to. They might not have ever known what a tramp they were raising if it wasn't for me. I put my feet up and clicked on the boob tube to a rerun of The Office. The perfect ending to a perfect day.

41

Martha

Painting days have become my favorite days of the week. Once again, I find myself in the back of my closet. The clothes I have stored there are from a lifetime ago. Bringing them out reminds me how much I used to love dressing up. I find a sundress I wore years ago when the boys were young. Surprisingly, it still fits, although a few spots are a little tighter than they used to be. I inspect myself in the full-length mirror on the back of our bedroom door. I look pretty darn good. After doing my hair and makeup, I slip on sandals that show off my newly painted toenails. If you don't look too closely, you would think they were done by a professional. I spritz my wrists and neck with my favorite jasmine body spray and head downstairs.

Walter glances up from his paper when I walk into the kitchen, and his chin nearly hits the table. "You're beautiful," he says, staring at me.

"This old thing?" I say, blushing.

He stands and wraps his arms around me. "And you smell good too," he whispers, then leans down and kisses me with a little more effort than the pecks we usually give each other.

"I might dress up more if I knew this would be your reaction." I giggle, feeling years younger than my actual age.

I walk to the park with a bounce in my step. The chairs and easels are set up, and Bonnie is waiting for me. Her floppy sun hat sits on the seat next to her. Her face lights up when she sees me.

"I saved you a spot." She beams with joy.

"Thank you." I place her hat back on her head before taking a seat.

"I love your dress," Bonnie says, her grin growing.

"This old thing?" I smile, secretly happy she noticed my effort. She is the reason I dressed up. Walter's reaction was a bonus.

Our instructor directs us to take a closer look at the display set up in the middle of the circle of easels. Different fruits sit in a bright blue bowl, and several vases hold a variety of brilliantly colored flowers. Various sticks and rocks cover the rest of the table. She tells us we will be painting a still life. I've never done one before, but I feel up to the challenge and get to work.

"How have you been?" I whisper to Bonnie after organizing my supplies.

"I've been good. Busy with the usual stuff. Cleaning, laundry, cooking. It seems it doesn't matter how old you get; you still gotta do all the mundane chores," Bonnie sighs.

"Did you ever have another job? Besides the thankless job of being a full-time mother, maid, and everything everyone else needs?"

I hope she appreciates my sense of humor. I want to make sure I don't do all the talking this time. It is my day to listen, so I can prove to Bonnie what a good friend I am. Last night before I fell asleep, I made a list of possible questions in my head. I don't want to run out of things to ask her.

"My main job was the thankless, never-ending job of being everything to everybody." She grins at me. I'm glad she acknowledged my joke. "I also worked as a part-time writer for the lifestyle section of the local paper. I covered everything they thought a woman would want to read: cooking, child care, cleaning tips, department store openings, and local family activities. I should have been offended by the fact they never gave me any real news to cover, but my job was easy, so I didn't mind. But do you want to know the truth?" she asks, eyes twinkling.

I nod my head yes, excited she is going to share a secret with me.

"My real dream was to write a mystery novel. I have many notebooks filled with the beginnings of great works of fiction. The trouble is, I never finished any of them. I may be great at beginnings, but I stink at endings. It's funny because the main character had young children when I started writing my first book. In the second book, the kids were in high school. On my next attempt, the kids were in college. Looking back on it now, I realize I was writing about my life, and that's why I never had an ending. I wanted the story to go on forever. Great for my life, but not so great for a reader. I should start a new book. A new friendship takes hold when two amazing older women take a painting class together, become fast friends, and then take down a neighborhood killer, all while baking the perfect apple pie." She grins at me and bursts out laughing.

I join in her laughter. Too many years have passed since I have had a friend to share stories with. I didn't realize how much I missed connecting to someone other than Walter.

42

Walter

As soon as Martha is out the door, I grab three hundred dollars from the desk drawer and hurry to the senior center. All they have left are boring glazed donuts. I take three and devour them in the car on my way to the hardware store. My mission is to buy the four panels for the rest of the fence project and a faucet for the bathroom.

The traffic light in front of the grocery store is red. Since I have to stop anyway, I might as well run in and grab a couple of scratchers. When I win, I will take Martha out for a special dinner. She looked stunning this morning. I must be the luckiest man alive to have a wife who gets more beautiful with age.

"Good morning, sugar. Do you have some winners to cash out today?" Fran greets me with her perfect smile.

"My last tickets were all defective, but I think with a little help, we can turn that around. How about you pick me five one-dollar winners." I lay a five-dollar bill on the counter.

"I will try. However, I have no idea which ones are winners and which ones are losers."

When Fran hands me the tickets her hand brushes mine. My

skin tingles with her touch. I jog out to my car. Funny how being around Fran makes my hip feel better. Once I settle in the worn seat, I get to scratching. The first two are defective, but the third is a one-dollar winner. I'm back in the game. The fourth is a five-dollar winner. The last one is a fifty-dollar winner. Woo hoo! I knew it was my lucky day. I can take Martha to dinner and have a little left over. Too bad I need to finish this fence project before Martha gets home, or I would go back to thank Fran for picking winners. For now, I put them in the pocket of my cargo shorts and head to the hardware store.

While perusing the fence panels, a kid appears and stands next to me.

"Can I help you with something?" he asks.

He doesn't look a day over fifteen. However, he is wearing a store name tag on his shirt, so he must work here.

"Can I get four of those panels?" I ask him, pointing to the panels that match the ones I purchased at the ReStore.

"Sure thing. Want me to put them on a flatbed cart for you? I can help load them into your truck too," he offers.

"I don't have a truck, but I would appreciate the help. I need to purchase a faucet first, though."

The kid follows me to the faucets, talking non-stop.

"There is a girl that kind of likes me. Not sure if I really like her, but I like her enough that we could have some fun, if you know what I mean. The last thing I need is a relationship. I got big plans for my life. I'm gonna be a professional skateboarder. Travel the world. Can't tie me down, but she's pretty cute. I might hit it and quit it after a week or maybe a month."

I can hardly think with all his blabbering. The wall of faucets

is a bit daunting. I narrow it down to the few that are on clearance.
A polished nickel one is on clearance for sixty-five dollars. Martha
prefers brushed nickel. Of course, that style is not on clearance and
costs over one hundred dollars. You would think it was pure gold at
that price. Hopefully, she will be thankful the polished nickel faucet
doesn't leak like the old one and not worry about the finish. The
chatty stocker follows me up to the check-out lines, pushing the
panels in the flatbed cart, talking incessantly about nothing. I quit
listening back by the faucets.

The cashier tells me the total is $295.25 with tax. I hand her all
my cash and dig in my pocket for the change. A dime and six pennies
stare at me from my open palm.

The kid hands the cashier a dime. "I got you, bro," he smirks at
me.

"Thanks," I mumble, humiliated.

The kid follows me out to the car. He looks from the panels to
my car and shakes his head. "Bro, not gonna fit."

"Sure they will," I insist.

I open one of the rear doors and pull down the seats. After
I pop the trunk we grab a panel and attempt to place it in the car.
When that doesn't work, we try the side door, hoping the back seat
will hold them. I realize the annoying kid is right. No way are they
going to fit.

"Like I said, bro, not gonna fit. You need a truck."

"Well, BRO, as you can see, I don't have a truck," I say a bit too
loudly.

"Might need to rent one then, bro."

"I'm not your bro. I am old enough to be your grandfather.
Have some respect," I shout, flustered.

I trudge back into the store, and he follows with the cart. He starts talking about how his gramps used to take him fishing and taught him how to play cards. Now his gramps has dementia and can't remember who he is. I wish he would shut the hell up, so I could think.

"Gramps needs a truck," the kid says to the man behind the customer service desk.

The older gentleman narrows his eyes at the kid, shaking his head, then quickly turns towards me to ask how he can help me.

"I need to rent a truck."

"No problem, our trucks are $24.99 for three hours. I will need your ID and a major credit card for the deposit. You will get the entire deposit back if you return the truck in the same condition as when you rented it."

Well, this is a problem. Martha took control of the credit cards after I got into a little trouble ages ago. Thankfully I got lucky at the casino and paid the cards off in only a couple of months. It took years to prove to Martha I was a changed man.

"I don't have a credit card. Can I pay cash?" I ask.

He shakes his balding head. "I'm sorry, sir, I need a card for the security deposit. We can deliver your order right to your door for a forty-dollar charge. You can pay for that with cash if you would like."

"When can it be delivered?"

"We can have it delivered as early as this afternoon," he says, staring at the computer screen in front of him.

That won't work. Martha will be home and wonder why I didn't buy them all together.

"How about Thursday morning?" I ask.

"We can make that work. I just need forty dollars and an address."

"No problem. I'll need to return this first," I say, handing back the faucet.

He takes my receipt and hands me the cash I have left after the charge for the delivery—less than thirty dollars. There's no way I can get a decent faucet for that price. I leave empty handed.

I walk past the kid gathering carts in the parking lot. "Have a great day, bro," he calls. I resist the urge to punch him in his smug young face.

43

Journal

This afternoon was darn near perfect. The good Lord blessed me with a lovely breeze and less humidity, making the dreadful heat bearable. Sitting on my front porch, I read my book and sipped my sweet peach tea. The neighborhood was quiet except for the happy sounds of kids playing in the sprinkler over yonder.

I was minding my own business, lost in the thriller I was reading. Don't you love it when a book takes you to a new world with lots of twists and turns to keep you on your toes? Now mind you, I knew who had done it less than halfway in. I was thinking I can't wait for the end to prove I'm right when I heard a child screeching like a rabbit about to be dinner.

I looked down the street to where the horrible noise was coming from. It was that sweet boy, Charlie. His donkey of a daddy was yelling at him, even called him a brat. Can you imagine calling that tiny child a brat? My chest was so tight I thought the good Lord was calling me home.

The next thing I knew, the monster was chasing after Charlie, who was running for his life. The evil beast caught up to him, grabbed his pint-sized body, and hurled him back toward his house. The precious child sailed through the air, landing hard on a huge rock by my neighbor's half-dead shrubs. I heard a snap with my own two ears, and then another ear-

shattering scream. You wouldn't believe what came out of that horrible man's mouth next. He told Charlie to look at what he made him do. He even made him apologize. Tears streamed down Charlie's dirty little cheeks.

Can you believe that monster blaming his son for his terrible temper? I was mad as a mule chewing on bumblebees. The good-for-nothing scum leaned down to tell Charlie the plan. In a voice low as the snake he is, he told Charlie to tell the doctor and his mama that he hurt himself running and that his nice daddy was right there to take care of him. Even promised him a treat to seal the deal on his deceitful plan. Then the vermin picked the tiny child up by his other arm and looked around, making sure no one had seen what he did. I quickly tucked myself behind my ivy-covered trellis before he could see me. If only I weren't such a scaredy cat. I should have been strong enough to stand up to the likes of him. Now I understand why his wife doesn't stand up to him. That man is nothing but pure evil.

As soon as the coast was clear, I went straight inside my house to come up with a plan. Pacing the kitchen and living room, I was sweating like a hooker in church. My heart was damn near pounding out of my chest. A splash of ice-cold water from the sink and some deep breaths was the only thing that brought me back to reality. I bet my therapist would be proud of me.

I needed to weigh my options with a clear mind. If I had called the police, the patrol car would've shown up at my house for a statement. The whole neighborhood, including that prick, would know I called. That might make things worse for little Charlie. What if they took him away? He would end up in foster care, and his mama would never forgive me. I couldn't take it if I caused her more pain than she was already in. Another idea popped into my head to call the hospital and tell them what I had seen. They might not believe me, though. If they questioned the little guy in front of his evil daddy, Charlie might get a beating even worse if he got his story wrong.

My old brain was running on empty when I remembered the "See something, Say something" commercial for Child Protective Services. They said you could file an anonymous claim. The ad was so precious, all the lovely children playing with happy parents looking on. Made me feel like all the horrible parents had been eradicated from the earth, creating a utopia of goodness and joy.

I started up my laptop right then and there and typed in North Carolina Child Protective Services. The form was simple to fill out—date, time, and exactly what I witnessed. It was easy to portray Dave as the swine he is. I described in detail how he threw that precious child. Don't you worry now. I didn't forget to include a paragraph about how Ashley is a great mama and takes real good care of Charlie. At the bottom was a space for contact information if you wanted an update on the outcome of your claim. They promised that the person you are turning in wouldn't be made privy to your info, so I filled out my name and email address.

It's only a matter of time until Ashley and Charlie will be safe. All thanks to me

44

Martha

Walter's headache has him sleeping in this morning. I creep in and gather his dirty laundry. His favorite cargo shorts, so caked with grime, they could stand on their own, are thrown carelessly on my beautiful floral chair. How hard is it to put your dirty clothes in the hamper? Additional offensive articles from Walter's wardrobe are on the floor behind the bathroom door. You would not believe all the places I find his soiled laundry.

After the first load is in the machine, I go back upstairs to confirm I didn't miss any of his filthy clothes. Would you believe it? The stench from his shorts still lingers in the room. The odor attached itself to my chair. I douse the chair with Febreeze and cross my fingers that the magical chemicals will work. Behind the chair, I find his community officer shirt and remember to unpin his badge. It appears more professional seeing it up close in the light of day.

Three pieces of thick paper are at the bottom of the wash bin when I transfer the first load from the washer to the dryer. I scold myself for not going through his pockets before throwing the clothes in the washing machine. Upon closer inspection, I realize they are instant lottery tickets.

Decades ago Walter had a gambling problem at the local casino and lost quite a bit of money. When I found out about it a big fight ensued. He had racked up a lot of credit card debt leaving me blindsided and feeling betrayed. Our marriage might have been over if it wasn't for his promise that he would no longer gamble at the casino.

The first thing I did was cancel the credit cards. I kept the gas card and one credit card in my name for emergencies. Walter took some initiative and scheduled weekly appointments with a therapist he found in the yellow pages. She specialized in gambling addiction. Our health insurance at the time didn't cover much, but we both agreed the seventy-five dollar weekly visit charge was worth it. He picked up extra shifts at the mall on weekends and did a couple of evening security jobs for a local venue to earn the money. After a couple of months, the therapist told him he was cured.

I still didn't fully trust him so I continued to monitor his spending closely. A few years after the incident, Walter's wealthy cousin and his wife visited from California. We ran out of things to do by the second day and didn't want them to be bored so we took them to the casino. Walter promised not to gamble and he stuck to his word. It wasn't until then that I could fully trust him. He had overcome his problem and saved our marriage in the process.

It was a relief to hand the bills over to Walter again. I did enough record-keeping at my job and I certainly didn't enjoy doing it at home too. The recipe for a successful marriage is trust and compromise.

Since Walter still loved an occasional scratcher I would buy him a few for his Christmas stocking. Every once in a while, I snuck one under his pillow with a love note. Some time has passed since I bought him a scratcher or wrote him a love note.

I put the wet tickets on a towel in the guest bathroom to dry, hoping he can still turn them in if they were winners, and decide to buy him a few replacements for the ones I ruined.

The pleasant lotto cashier greets me with a warm smile as I walk up to the counter, "How can I help you today, sugar?"

She is so personable and sweet. I bet everyone thinks she's in love with them.

"Three one-dollar scratchers, please. You pick," I say, setting a five-dollar bill on the counter.

"Sure thing, sweetie. Best of luck. I have a feeling you're going to get lucky." If I didn't know better, I would think she was flirting with me.

45

Fran

Another dull day at the lotto counter. I second guess my life choices as one elderly person after another blows their retirement savings and kid's inheritance in ten seconds scratching a little gray square. As I daydream of tearing every last one of those dreaded tickets to shreds, my prick of a neighbor with his son in tow comes through the doors. The little guy tenderly holds the cast with his good arm as his asshole daddy leads him to the ice cream aisle.

"Pick out anything you like," Dave's voice carries through the store.

"Now tell Daddy thank you." I hear him say when they are in the checkout lane.

"Thank you, Daddy," the sweet boy says in a tiny voice.

A knot forms in my stomach. As they walk out, the prick has the nerve to smile and wave at me. I quickly turn away. There is no way I'll give him the satisfaction of thinking his pathetic display of fake parenting is okay in my book. My hands form into fists, my nails digging into my palms. That asshole needs to be stopped. As I take a deep breath to calm my nerves, I hear, "Excuse me, Excuse me," and I am brought back to reality by another blue hair that needs a lotto ticket.

"Hope you get lucky," I say with my best fake smile.

46

Walter

My head still hurts when I wake up. It's no wonder between that kid never shutting up and having to return the faucet. The ibuprofen from last night has worn off. I shuffle to the bathroom to pop four more in my mouth, take a drink from the leaky faucet to wash it down, and head straight back to bed.

When I open my eyes several hours later, my lotto tickets are the first thing that pops into my mind. The clothes I was going to put back on are missing. I race downstairs in my underwear, hoping Martha hasn't finished the laundry. Please let me find them before she goes through the pockets or throws them in the washer. A load of towels sits freshly washed in the washing machine. The dryer is still warm. I swing the door open, grab my favorite shorts and search the pockets. Empty. I throw them on as my headache returns. Just like that, fifty-six dollars down the drain.

Trudging up the stairs, I decided now would be as good a time as any to see how much money is left in the secret drawer. I call for Martha—no response. At least I can check the money situation without her prying eyes. I grab the envelope and count the small pile of bills—forty dollars. How can this be? The money vanished so quickly. I still need a new faucet and can't wait much longer to fix the air in the car. Yesterday, the tepid air blowing from the vents became downright sweltering.

I slip the money into my wallet and throw the envelope away. All I need is a big win. While Martha is at her class on Saturday, I can borrow a little money from the checking account. The bills aren't due for a couple of weeks, leaving plenty of time to return my winnings from the casino to the bank account.

As I walk to Frank's house to grab the golf cart for my community officer shift I imagine my big win. The bells will ring, and all eyes will be on me when the attendant comes over to count the money into my open palm. It's nice to have the relief of a solid plan in place.

In the weekly neighborhood report, the lead officer told us to keep an eye on Dave's house. There is suspicion that he may be abusing his son. We are given strict orders not to confront him, just buzz by his house often so he's aware we are watching. If we have reasonable suspicions of abuse, we must report it immediately.

Driving around the neighborhood slowly, I notice what each family is doing. At Dave's house, his little boy, Charlie, is drawing with chalk on the driveway. He has a cast on one of his arms. His mom, Ashley, sits in a chair holding an open book, but her eyes are glued to little Charlie. When I drive by, she waves, and Charlie looks up from his drawing.

"Good afternoon, ma'am," I say as I pull the golf cart to the end of their driveway. "Hey, sport, nice cast. I bet you have a fun story of how you got it." Charlie gets up and runs to hide behind his mom.

"Sorry. Charlie's a bit shy. He was running and tripped on a rock and fell. Need to bubble wrap this one," she laughs nervously.

"Kids will be kids. I'm always around if you ever need help from the community officer. We know first aid." I hold up the red first aid bag. "We are here to support our community and keep everyone safe."

"Thanks. I will keep that in mind."

"I live a few houses down the street and can be here in less than a minute if you need assistance," I tell her, pointing in the direction of my house. She thanks me for the information, and Charlie manages a wave.

The day seems peaceful and quiet, so I spend the next hour making loops around the neighborhood, waving to any neighbors who are out and about. Each time I circle back, I wave to little Charlie. By the third time around, he is waving back to me. His father better not be abusing him because I will not stand for anyone hurting a child.

47

Martha

Walter is gone when I get back from the store. I quickly grab a scrap of paper from the junk drawer to write him a note.

Are you feeling lucky? These took a little ride in the washer, so I bought you a couple of replacements. I hope you can still cash in your winners.
Love, Martha.

After making the bed, I tuck the note, his washed scratchers, and the new scratchers under his pillow. Let's hope the lotto lady is right about getting lucky. Maybe a kiss like yesterday is in my future. Or maybe something even better.

48

Walter

Dinner is on the table when I return from my shift. I would have been home sooner, but Frank convinced me to look at his new fishing lures. Then he wouldn't shut up about them. After dinner, Martha and I watch a movie on Lifetime. I can't concentrate on the sappy stupid love story. Thoughts of my soon-to-be winnings swirl in my mind. The only other thought that creeps in is of little Charlie and his broken arm. I do hope his mom will reach out if I can help.

When the credits roll, I yawn and tell Martha I'm calling it a night. I am surprised when she clicks off the TV and follows me up the stairs. Maybe she wants to read in bed before she falls asleep. Glad the day is over; I stretch out in bed. While fluffing my pillow, my hand touches something. I pull out some paper. My heart nearly stops when I realize I'm holding my winning scratchers. Martha is gazing at me from her side of the bed. Holy crap, she knows about the scratchers. I search her face for anger, but all I see is a sly, sweet smile.

"Were they winners? I accidentally washed them. I am so sorry. Do you think you can still cash them in?" she asks with nothing but kindness in her voice.

Relief washes over me as my pulse returns to normal. Martha is concerned about washing my scratchers, not the fact that I had them in the first place. Quickly reading the note she left, I realize she has even bought me a couple of new ones. I am a lucky man to have such an understanding wife.

Looking into her eyes, I take her hand in mine. "They were winners, but don't worry about it. You are my real winner, and maybe they will still take them. Thank you for buying me some new tickets."

"You have worked so hard around our home and for our community. You earned them. Do you want to scratch them now?" She has a twinkle in her eye and is wearing my favorite nightgown.

I set the tickets on my nightstand and whisper, "They can wait," before I lean in to kiss her.

49

Journal

My palms were sweating like a toddler trying to hold onto a goldfish. I sent up a little prayer to the heavens for good news when I opened my email. Wouldn't you know it, the top email was from CPS. They said they were processing my claim. For Pete's sake, they made it sound like the boy's life was an order from Amazon.

Don't you worry, I'm keeping my eyes on that precious boy. His mama also seems to be keeping her eyes on him. She is right by his side whenever he's outside. His no-good daddy hasn't been around, making me hope my email worked. I'm giddy as a kid on Christmas Eve. Maybe that good-for-nothing is already rotting in jail where he belongs.

I tried on my funeral attire. It will be the perfect outfit to wear in court. I can't wait to testify and fry his ass.

50

Martha

I wake up rejuvenated. My cheeks feel warm as I think of the exciting evening Walter and I had last night. My elation fades when I look out the window to see the steady rain. The news confirms a soggy day ahead. No class today. I text Bonnie a sad face emoji.

She sends back an emoji of a store, a bag of cash, and a question mark. A few moments later, another text comes through.

I can pick you up in an hour for some retail therapy. We can turn that frown upside down.

I can't remember the last time I've been shopping for something other than groceries. Probably last Christmas. Unless something breaks, I don't need anything. I smile at the prospect of a shopping day with Bonnie and maybe finding something special for me.

Taking a little cash from the money Walter took out of our Christmas account is warranted. After all, I work day in and day out to keep our home in order, and I deserve to treat myself. I check every drawer on the desk. The envelope is nowhere. Walter is still sleeping, and I don't want to bother him yet. He's probably tired out from our fun night. I'll let him sleep while I prepare for a day of shopping with Bonnie. She always looks so put together, and I want to look my best. A floral sundress and a little makeup make me smile at my reflection in the mirror. Not bad for someone my age.

When Walter finally makes his way to the kitchen, I pour him a cup of coffee.

"My class is canceled today because of the rain. Bonnie invited me to go shopping. I was going to take a couple of twenties, but I couldn't find the envelope in the desk. Did you move it?"

His good mood from last night leaves his face. He hates when I go shopping. He wears the same thing every day; old cargo shorts and a twenty-year-old t-shirt, and he thinks I should do the same.

"You must have missed the envelope. I'm sure it's right where I left it." He pulls out his wallet. "I have some cash you can use. How much do you think you will need?" he asks.

"How about forty dollars? If I don't spend it all I will put it towards groceries this week. How are we doing with the bills this month?"

"We are doing right as rain. Don't go on a crazy spending spree, though," he says, handing me the cash.

"Will do." I slip on my rain jacket and sit on the porch to wait for Bonnie.

51

Walter

That was a close call. I'm glad I put the rest of the money from the desk in my wallet. What would Martha think if she saw we only had forty dollars left? Thanks to her spur-of-the-moment shopping spree, all the money's gone. At least she won't be home when the fence panels are delivered.

While Martha waits for her friend on the porch, I open the laptop on the kitchen table. Time to check the bank balance. Most of our money is in investments that we can't touch yet. We need to sit on them for a while to ensure our retirement will last at least thirty more years. When the time comes, I want to be able to take care of Martha with top-of-the-line nursing care. We can't count on our boys to help. They have their own lives and expenses living in the big city.

We live on our social security, and it's not a problem most months. We can pay the bills and buy groceries. Martha has a personal savings account worth about five thousand dollars from the sale of her parent's home. They didn't have much of an estate left after she paid off their past medical expenses. She said she wanted to keep it separate to use it if we ever got into a bind with our medical expenses or the boys needed some help. I'm not so sure those were her motives. I think she liked having it in case she ever wanted to hitch her horse to a different wagon, if you know what I mean. Throughout our marriage, she refused to touch her money, causing us to refinance the house to help pay for the boys' college. She was pretty smug when she found out I had spent some of our savings on gambling. "At least I have my money," she bragged. That was in the middle of my unlucky streak, but like always, I was able to turn it around.

I open her account. Her balance is $5,526, meaning she's made $526 in interest. It's too bad she didn't invest this in a higher-yield account, but Martha likes to play things safe. Has she realized it has gone up in value? I won't touch her money, although I'm glad it's there, just in case. The mortgage isn't due for a couple of weeks, so it won't be a problem to take a couple hundred out of our joint account for the casino on Saturday. You can't win if you don't play is my motto.

The delivery truck pulls up five minutes after Martha's friend picks her up. Perfect timing. The kid from the hardware store is with the truck driver and starts talking as soon as he opens the door.

"This house is fire," he yells.

I quickly turn and search for smoke. There is none. This kid is an idiot.

"Wish my granny had a house this nice. I would move in with her for sure. Did I tell ya that you remind me of my gramps? I bet before he got dementia, you two would have really liked each other."

Ignoring the kid, I direct the driver to set the panels near the old ones. The rain needs to stop before I can get them in place. Using my power tools in the rain is plain stupid. Within minutes the panels are unloaded, and loud rap music fills the air as the driver starts the truck. The kid walks up to me with the delivery slip.

"Hey bro, here's your paperwork. You got a tip for me?"

"I sure do. Learn to be quiet. You talk too much. Also, don't hook up with a girl you don't want a relationship with. Women get real mad when they feel used. You ever hear the saying, 'Hell hath no fury like a woman scorned?' Don't be a jerk. Be someone your gramps and granny can be proud of." Grabbing the soggy paper from him, I turn and walk into the house before he can respond.

52

Martha

"Thanks for picking me up," I tell Bonnie, pulling off my hood as I settle in her dry car.

"No problem. Thanks for going with me."

We drive in silence as I rack my brain to come up with something witty to say.

"How is your daughter doing?" I finally ask, giving up on being clever.

"She's doing better. Her good-for-nothing husband left for a while to work with his brother downstate. I think he left because he broke my grandson's arm and wanted to get out of town before the authorities came to pick him up."

Bonnie grips the steering wheel so tightly her knuckles turn white. Another driver cuts her off, narrowly missing my door. A string of curse words tumble out of her mouth as if a drunken sailor has possessed her body.

"Sorry," she apologizes. "I'm so angry."

"I understand, I would be angry too. On a positive note, this rain will be good for the flowers," I try to lighten the mood.

"That asshole bought Ashley flowers and treats for Charlie. Like that makes up for his violence," she hisses. "The way he pretends to be decent makes him seem more like the snake in the grass I know he is. The only good thing is, with him gone for a while I can visit at least. This weekend, Charlie is staying at my house for movie night so Ashley can go and enjoy herself with her friend. I pray she sees there is a life outside of her horrible marriage and that other people care about her. Maybe she will get the courage to leave for good."

We turn a corner and see several signs for an estate sale.

"Let's stop and find some treasures!" Bonnie turns her head towards me with a hopeful look in her eyes.

"I haven't been to an estate sale in years. Now that I'm an old lady, I find I don't need any old lady stuff." I laugh.

"You're not old—you're vintage." Bonnie smirks. "Come on. I love to get a first-hand look into other people's lives. I create a documentary film in my head. Maybe I will be inspired to create the perfect novel AND finish it this time. Or maybe we will find a treasure worth millions, and then we can go on *Antiques Roadshow* and act shocked when they tell us our find is priceless. We'll split the millions and travel the world together without a care in the world."

"Now you're talking. Okay, let's do it," I agree.

We follow the signs to the sale. Cars line the street. Bonnie finds the closet spot, which isn't as close as I would like with the current weather conditions.

"Looks like the whole town is here. Let's run for it," Bonnie shouts and dashes out her door.

We giggle like school girls as we race for the entrance. Under the shelter of the garage, we laugh so hard we have to cross our legs.

Bonnie points to a dead tree in the corner of the garage. "Master gardener, I see," she manages to say through her laughter.

"She might have been missing her green thumb," I reply, making Bonnie laugh harder.

"How much for the lovely tree?" Bonnie asks an older gentleman who is pricing items.

"Five dollars," he responds with not even a hint of a smile.

"I don't think that will be worth a million on the *Roadshow*," I tease.

"It is vintage, though." She laughs. "Look, her husband was a handyman," she says, picking up a hammer on a table full of tools.

"Or her wife," I say, pointing to a pride flag in the corner.

"Wow! She was hip before her time. Let's explore the rest of their lives inside."

We walk into the well-decorated home. Even with the display tables loaded with items, you can tell how beautiful the house is. Modern art lines the walls in the living room with Art Deco furniture to match the theme.

"I think one of them was a lawyer or a doctor," Bonnie guesses as she scans the room.

"Maybe a writer," I say, pointing to the bookshelves filled with books lining an entire wall behind her.

Her eyes grow wide as she turns around to see the large selection of hardcovers.

"A dream come true!" Bonnie clasps her hands together. "If it wasn't raining, I would take all of these."

We peruse the collection before heading to the kitchen. Every gadget known to man fills the countertops.

"One of them liked to cook," I say confidently.

A thin blonde woman pricing items chimes in, "They both do.

My aunts own a restaurant in downtown Asheville. Maybe you've heard of it—The Silver Spoon?"

"I have never been, but I bet the food is outstanding," Bonnie says.

"Yes. The food is amazing. You should check it out." She reaches into her apron pocket and hands us a coupon for twenty-five percent off. "I manage it for them. They took a break to hike through Europe to look for a spot to open a restaurant. I'm a bit jealous of their freedom," she says as two kids chase each other through the kitchen, arguing over who broke a vase in the basement.

She rolls her eyes and runs after the kids yelling, "I told you to leave everything alone! Why can't you behave for once?"

"So glad my kids are grown," Bonnie says when the coast is clear.

We continue the tour of the beautiful home. In one of the bedrooms, Bonnie plops down on a king-size bed full of pillows.

"I have never been so comfortable in my life," she sighs and pats the bed.

I lay on the other side, and she turns toward me.

"In our next life, this could be us." She smiles slyly.

"I do really like you but not like that," I tease.

"Maybe in your next life." Bonnie bats her eyes at me and smirks.

We look through the walk-in closet next. There is nothing I can afford with my meager budget. Even so, it never hurts to look. Bonnie gasps and hits my arm. Her eyes bulge at the store price tag still on a jacket.

"Who buys a jacket for over four hundred dollars and doesn't wear it?" I ask, shaking my head.

"I feel better about my Francesca's dress with the tags still on that's in my closet," she says, carefully returning the jacket to the rack.

Francesca's. I will remember to take a look at their website.

Bonnie waves me over to a table full of jewelry. Rows of sparkly rings for twenty dollars each. Finally, something we can afford.

"Let's each pick out a piece. With any luck, these will be our million-dollar *Roadshow* items. And if they're not worth anything, we will have something to remind us of our first shopping adventure," Bonnie says, carefully inspecting each ring.

I choose one with a ruby-colored gem surrounded by four diamonds.

"What are the chances this is real?" I ask Bonnie, holding the ring up to the light.

"If we were at my house, I would say zero. Here, I would guess fifty percent."

Bonnie decides on a brilliant sapphire gem surrounded by tiny glistening diamonds.

"This is the one for me. It will match my eyes," she says, holding the ring next to her face for me to admire.

We pay the cashier, and Bonnie suggests we use our coupon to have an elegant lunch at The Silver Spoon wearing our fancy rings. We run back to the car laughing, dodging raindrops along the way.

53

Walter

The rain drenched my shirt. I peel it off, throw it down the stairs in the vicinity of the washing machine, and head upstairs to retrieve a dry one. The lotto tickets Martha bought me sit on my nightstand with the remains of the ones that took a spin in the washer. I grab them all, go to the kitchen, and grab a paper clip from the junk drawer. The first two are defective. The third one has a matching winning number. Let it be a large prize amount, I silently pray. Five dollars—not great. With the doubler, I have a chance to double the amount. I slowly scratch the space to reveal the two-times icon. I did it—a ten-dollar winner.

Hopefully, Fran can cash in my washed tickets, making my total sixty-six dollars. Not bad for a day's work. I will tell her not to break the rules just for me. I don't want my lucky charm to get into trouble.

The senior center is conveniently on the way. A quick stop for donuts won't hurt. Jelly-filled today. I grab two, hoping for raspberry. They are a bit stale. That's what I get, I suppose. The early bird gets the worm and the fresh donuts. I devour them in the car, hunched over the dash. The gooey liquid (I can't tell which fruit it's supposed to be) drips onto the steering wheel. At least it didn't drip on my shirt. I want to look presentable.

Fran is helping someone with a return. She offers me a warm smile and mouths the words "I'm sorry" as I patiently wait my turn.

"Hello, sunshine, on my rainy day. Want to cash out some winners?" she asks as I approach.

"I do have some winners for you today, but a couple of them took a little ride in the washer. Can you still take them?" I ask hopefully.

"Were you trying to launder money?" She laughs at her joke and starts scanning the tickets. "Looks like the laundry didn't wash the luck out of them," she teases.

"Are you sure you won't get in trouble if you take them?"

"I'll tell you what, if my manager gives me a hard time and I lose this job, I will move in with you." She winks.

My face gets hot as I imagine her showing up on my doorstep with a suitcase. I'm jolted back to reality when she asks how I would like my cash.

"I'm on a roll, so let's keep it going. How about if you pick me some more winners? I'll take twelve five-dollar scratchers and a one-dollar scratcher."

Fran wishes me luck when she hands me the stack of tickets. I head to the car to get scratching. The first four are defective. Blood rushes to my head, and I wonder if I should have taken the cash. After a few deep breaths, my mind clears. For extra measure, I repeat my favorite mantra, "A win is right around the corner."

The next three are defective.

"A win is right around the corner," I repeat several times.

The eighth ticket is a five-dollar winner. Not great, but it's a start. The last four five-dollar scratchers are all defective—definitely a bad batch.

My last hope is the one-dollar ticket. I slowly scratch the numbers. One matches my lucky number revealing a one-dollar prize. Six dollars in winnings? Terrible. The defective cards go in the parking lot trash can. I slide the winners into my wallet, where they will be safe from the washing machine.

Time for a quick stop at the bank to get the money for my lucky day on Saturday. I pull out three hundred dollars. My balance reflects almost enough to cover the upcoming bills. I'll have plenty of time to replenish the account.

54

Martha

The rain stops, and the sun peeks out from behind the clouds as we pull into a parking space at The Silver Spoon. Bonnie points to a double rainbow arching across the sky when we step out of the car.

"It's a sign. Maybe we already found our pot of gold," Bonnie says, twirling her ring. "Let's visit my favorite pawn shop after lunch to see how we did," she suggests.

"You have a favorite pawn shop?" I ask.

"I sure do. Just in case I need to unload a gun or some diamonds," Bonnie says with a chuckle.

I laugh nervously and wonder if Bonnie isn't as carefree and sweet as she presents herself.

The restaurant is cozy, and the decor is tasteful. A young woman plays the violin, adding to the ambiance. We both order the harvest chicken salad with candied pecans and homemade balsamic dressing. When the server brings freshly baked bread with chive butter, Bonnie asks about the violin player.

"The owners like to support our community arts programs, so they hire local high school students to perform in the summer.

Yesterday two girls did a theatrical performance about getting their periods. We lost some male customers that day, but I thought it was informative and entertaining. Now, I better understand my mom and sisters," the server explains with a straight face.

We enjoy our lunch while listening to beautiful music. I love that neither of us has to make uncomfortable small talk to fill the space. We can purely enjoy each other's company. Bonnie dabs her eyes with her napkin.

"Are you okay?" I ask.

"Yes. The music is so beautiful. It reminds me of when my kids were young. So pure and lovely, untouched by the harshness of the world."

I pay my tab with the bank card and put my last twenty in the musician's tip jar. I want her to know how much I enjoyed her beautiful music. Walter would be upset if he knew I was giving away our money. He never understood charity. Bonnie also slides a twenty into the jar. The young lady stops playing for a moment to give us both a hug and thank us for our kindness.

Bonnie drives us to her favorite pawn shop after lunch. The door chimes our arrival. A man with a full beard, long hair, and arms covered in tattoos looks up from his phone.

"Well, hello, good to see you as always. What brings you in today?" he asks.

It's obvious they know each other. It is making me wonder if Bonnie has unloaded guns here.

"My best friend and I have some rings we would like appraised if you have the time," Bonnie informs him.

Bonnie called me her best friend. I stop myself from jumping for joy, but I can't hide the giant smile on my face.

"I always have time for you. Let me see what you have," he says with a big grin.

Bonnie hands her ring to him. He studies it for a moment, puts it under a magnifying glass to get a closer look, and punches some numbers into the laptop on the counter.

"I would guess this is worth about twenty-five dollars. It was made in mass for Macy's and sold for under fifty dollars in 1995. It's costume jewelry, so unfortunately not worth a lot. However, it does match your eyes." He winks at Bonnie.

He turns his attention to my ring and studies it under the magnifying glass. Bringing out a laser tool, he points the red beams at the gems. He grins sheepishly and tells me the gems appear genuine and of good quality. After he types something into his laptop, he swivels the computer to show me a picture.

"The designer is from Italy. This design was created in the early 2000s and is a limited edition. I would gladly take the ring off your hands for five hundred dollars."

"If he says he will buy it for five hundred, you can bet it's worth at least double that, if not triple," Bonnie says, taking the ring and handing it back to me.

I slide the ring back on my finger and marvel at its beauty.

"I'm Deaven, by the way," he says, handing me a business card. "Come back when you want to sell, and I will gladly assist you."

"Are you going to do any shopping today?" he asks Bonnie.

"Nope, not today. Please give my best to your mom, though."

"I certainly will. Bye Aunt Bonnie and Aunt Bonnie's best friend. See you soon. If you want to unload anything, I'm your man."

"Aunt Bonnie, I see why this is your favorite pawn shop," I say, getting into the car.

"My nephew has been through some hard times, but he's a good kid. He worked hard and was able to create a profitable business. I support him whenever I can. Are you going to sell your ring?" she asks.

"I think I want to keep it. It will remind me of our amazing day," I say, admiring my ring. "Plus, I thought we were going to take our treasures to the *Antiques Roadshow?*"

"Practice your surprise face." Bonnie glances at me as she drives.

"It's worth what? I can't believe it!" I shout, making a strange face. We both burst into laughter.

"You might want to work on that. You're not quite ready for TV yet," she teases.

55

Walter

The rain stops on my way home from the bank. Perfect timing to get to work installing the new fence panels. The process is more challenging by myself, but I manage to finish in under two hours. I stack the old panels next to the garage to break down later. Putting a few pieces in the trash can each week might take a month or so, but it's cheaper than a trip to the dump.

My stomach growls, and I look at my watch. It's after one o'clock already. Martha must have stopped for lunch with her friend, so I guess I'll have to fend for myself. The fridge is almost bare. I scour the cupboards for my favorite canned meat. The only thing I find is canned vegetables, a dented can of kidney beans, and half a jar of peanut butter. A peanut butter sandwich isn't as good as a gourmet sandwich with spicy mustard and dill, but it will have to do. My luck turns around when I find half a bag of chips in the pantry behind the old canning jars. I better go with Martha on the next shopping trip to stock up on my special supplies for a situation like this. At least I can eat in front of the television without getting in trouble.

56

Martha

Walter is asleep on the couch, covered in potato chip crumbs. The empty bag lies on the floor next to his feet. Normally I would be ticked off due to the extra work he has created for me and his lack of impulse control. However, today was such a great day that I can't be mad. I take the chip bag and his plate to the kitchen and wait for him to wake up so I can tell him about my fun day.

When he finally comes into the kitchen, I wave my hand in front of his face. He inspects my ring.

"How much did this set us back?" he grumbles.

"You'll never believe it! Only twenty dollars! Bonnie took me to her nephew Deaven's pawn shop. He said he would give me five hundred dollars for it. Bonnie said that means it's worth two or three times that amount. Can you believe it? I spent twenty dollars, and my ring could be worth fifteen hundred!" I can barely contain my excitement.

"Do you want to sell it? We could use the money for a little vacation or something fun like car repairs," he suggests.

"I thought you pulled the money from the Christmas saving

account for the car repairs." The excitement over my fun day is fading.

"Don't worry, dear. I have it covered. I just thought something else was bound to come up, and I didn't think you were really into flashy jewelry."

"I'm not normally into jewelry, but this ring is worth more than its monetary value. It will remind me of my lovely day with Bonnie. When *Antiques Roadshow* comes to town, Bonnie said she would go with me to get it appraised. We'll be stars on TV."

"You're already a star to me." Walter holds my hand up to the light to get a better look at my ring. "It is beautiful but not as beautiful as the woman wearing it." He gives me a peck on my cheek.

57

Martha

Almost no food is in the house, not a single egg or a drop of milk. I should go to the store before Walter wakes up, but I hate going first thing in the morning. At this time of day, the store is filled with old people who can't make up their minds or forget why they came to the store in the first place. With my luck, Walter would wake up, remember the ten things he thought he needed, and call me while I was trying to shop. I will shop right before dinner and grab one of those pre-cooked chickens. That way, I will avoid annoying elderly shoppers, and I won't have to cook.

"Two birds, one stone," I inform the cat, purring at my feet.

I take the pad off the fridge and start making a list. Walter shuffles into the kitchen with an overzealous yawn, interrupting my thoughts of what to prepare for meals this week. The weather is too hot to use the oven. I wish Walter liked salad as much as he likes my winter soups.

Walter pours a bowl of cereal before I have the chance to tell him there's no milk. I allow him to figure it out for himself, but not before he lets all the cold air out of the fridge, just staring as if milk will magically appear. He proceeds to pour his cereal back into the box, dumping most of it on the floor. I roll my eyes and grab the broom to sweep it up. It's easier to do it right the first time than to let him do it wrong and repeat the process later when he's not home. He finally discovers the waffles in the freezer and proceeds to make another mess.

I give up on the grocery list, open the laptop, and type Francesca's into the google search. Time to steal a bit of Bonnie's style. It is never too late to reinvent yourself, right? Walter plops down beside me and looks over my shoulder at the screen. His morning breath, mixed with maple syrup, makes me want to scream. Walter continues breathing heavily over my shoulder, so I suggest he watch the news. Maybe they will feature a crime he'll want to solve. Nothing major, mind you. But it was lovely when he was gone searching for that missing teacher for three days.

The television blares in the living room, and finally, I can relax—time to focus on fashion. The clothes are pretty and not as expensive as I thought they would be. I recognize the outfit Bonnie wore on the first day of painting class. Thankfully my memory is still sharp. She might think I'm a crazy stalker if I showed up as her twin. A couple of cute dresses make their way into my cart.

The television goes silent, so I quickly close the laptop. I don't need any prying eyes.

"Is it going to rain today?" I ask when Walter walks into the kitchen.

"The meteorologist said there is a fifty percent chance."

I don't like those odds, so I go out to water my plants. Walter follows me outside like a stray dog looking for food. He asks if I need any help. Since we only have one hose, I say no and continue watering. He wanders around the yard picking up a couple of sticks. It's already hot. Time to grab a glass of water and sit down with my book for a few minutes to recover from the heat. Walter comes back into the house as soon as I prop my feet on the coffee table.

"What are you reading?" he asks.

I pretend not to hear him. What's the point in telling him the name of a book he will never read?

58

Walter

Another dull morning with nothing to do.

"Going to the store today?" I ask Martha, who's sitting at the table making a grocery list.

She doesn't even look up to acknowledge me.

"Want me to go with you?" I try again.

"You can if you want. It's up to you."

Someone woke up on the wrong side of the bed. I guess I'm in charge of my own breakfast today.

I pour Special K into a bowl before realizing there's no milk. When I pour the cereal back into the box, half ends up on the floor. They shrunk the boxes, ripping everyone off and making the box openings way too small. Martha grabs the broom to clean up my mess. She loves to take care of me. While my waffles brown in the toaster, I ask if she can add a few things to the shopping list. She scribbles them on the pad and then opens the laptop. My antennae go up, and I casually ask what she's doing on the internet.

"Just looking around," she replies.

"Anything fun?" I ask and sit next to her.

"Nope. Checking emails. Boring stuff."

She angles the laptop away from me but I can see the screen in the reflection of her glasses. She's shopping again. I'm glad she's not checking the bank account but come on, how many outfits can one person wear? She only has one body.

59

Journal

When I finally had a chance to check my email, the first one, right there on the top, was from CPS. I figured it was a court date, so you can imagine my surprise when I started reading. They said they closed the case! They didn't do a darn thing to protect that sweet boy Charlie. No jail time for his good-for-nothing daddy. Not even a fine. The least they could have done is order him to go to a head shrinker or an anger management class. Nope. Case closed. I bet they never even opened the case. Well, I will be watching, and if he dares harm that boy again, he'd be wise to give his heart to Jesus because his ass will be mine.

60

Martha

Today will be another scorcher, according to the weather report. I wear stretchy capri shorts and a loose-fitting t-shirt. I want to be able to move freely during my self-defense class.

Walter is already drinking his coffee at the table when I walk into the kitchen. I didn't think he even knew how to work the coffee maker.

"Morning sunshine, ready to kick some butt and take some names?" He makes a karate-chopping move with his arm at the cat, who looks at him and then walks away unimpressed.

"You're up early," I say, pouring a cup of coffee.

I can tell from the sight and smell that it won't be as good as when I make the coffee.

"I want to get a jump on the day," he says, looking at me expectantly.

He's hoping I'll ask what he'll be up to while I'm in class. I don't feel like listening to him go on about how he's planning to clean the gutters or dethatch the lawn.

I respond, "Glad you are excited for the day," and pop my bread in the toaster.

As I take the last bite of my breakfast, he comes into the kitchen with his shoes on and asks if I'm ready to go.

"It's a bit early, isn't it?" I ask, glancing at the clock on the wall.

"Thought you liked to be early."

"I do. Just not this early."

I go upstairs to finish getting ready. When I come back down, Walter is already in the car. I guess this is better than being late.

61

Walter

Last night I dreamt of winning a new car at the casino, which should have been a dream come true. When I told Martha we now owned a state-of-the-art Lexus, she was furious. Can you believe that? Who wouldn't be happy with a shiny new fancy car?

It took me a couple of minutes to figure out the coffee maker. A few too many buttons, but it makes a fine cup of joe. Martha came down wearing the old college t-shirt our oldest son gave her years ago when he was in college. She looks cute. She didn't even ask me what I was doing today. Not that I would tell her; however, it would be nice to be asked. I took the time to concoct a story about cleaning the gutters. The last time it rained, water poured over the sides because they were so clogged. Oh well, it's better not to have to lie.

I want to drop Martha off at her class as early as possible. The sooner I can get to the casino, the more I will win.

62

Martha

Walter drops me off at the community center before the front doors are unlocked. He left so fast he didn't even notice that I couldn't get in. At least it's a lovely morning to sit outside to wait. Ten minutes pass before Titus shows up.

"Good morning. So glad you're here before anyone else," he greets me warmly.

I follow him to the door and wait for him to explain why he is glad I'm there before anyone else, but he doesn't continue. He flips on the lights in the lobby.

"The coffee is on a timer, so it should be ready. Would you care for a cup?" Titus asks.

"That would be lovely, thank you," I reply.

Titus walks to the kitchen at the back of the gym and returns with two cups of coffee along with a handful of cream, and sugar packets. I doctor mine up and take a sip. Titus' coffee is much better than the brown water Walter brewed, and the company is better too.

"How are you enjoying the class?" he asks.

"I love it. I am stronger and have more self-confidence. It's amazing all we have accomplished in only two classes."

"I'm glad to hear that," he smiles. "Every class I teach is different because the students control so much of the experience. If they are excited to learn and willing to try new things, it's a successful class. If they are closed-minded, well, I don't think I need to give you an example," he trails off and grins. "Some people fear embarrassment or injury, while others become risk-takers as they age. The latter feel like they have nothing to lose as they approach the end of their lives, so they might as well try everything. Other people become overly cautious, trying to ward off death so they won't try anything. They would rather sit home in a safety bubble than risk getting hurt. What kind of person are you?" he asks.

"I think I am a mix of both. There are days when nothing beats reading a book and sipping sweet tea. But I also love the adrenaline of hiding in the bushes and scaring the crap out of Julie," I chuckle. "Let me guess; you're a risk taker?"

"I used to be a huge risk taker. So much so that I ruined my marriage. My wife was tired of my dangerous stunts and driving too fast with her in the car. I would leave for hours or even days while she was home worrying about me. I wasn't a good communicator back then. Now I am more like you, Martha." Titus smiles at me.

I feel my blood pumping, and it feels fantastic. I haven't felt this alive in years.

I smile back as he continues, "I learned that I was taking risks with my health and body to avoid having a real relationship. I would jump off a cliff to avoid getting my heart broken. The military teaches you to take risks, to be brave, and not to have feelings. It took me years to be deprogrammed and learn how to be a civilian again. I chose to teach these classes differently. I enjoy helping people become more confident so they can go out in the world and be brave enough to stand up for themselves or to ask for help if they can't do it alone."

"Do you think you will get married again?" I ask.

"Maybe. I do know one thing for certain. I will do things differently if I get the opportunity to try again."

The class begins to file in, and I'm disappointed our conversation has to end.

63

Walter

I pop into the senior center before heading to the casino and snag two apple fritters. It's going to be a good day.

The casino parking lot is already quite packed. There are no spots near the entrance doors; I'll need to park in one of the outer lots. I snap a picture of the nearest pole marker and count the rows as I walk to the closest entrance. I push open the shiny gold doors, and the sight and smell of pure adrenaline greet me.

I'll warm up with slots. Once I'm hot, I'll play table games. Scanning the room, I see a crowd and hear cheers. A hot machine means another is near, so I head in that direction. I find an empty chair next to a young lady wearing a "Bride to be" sash. Her hot pink tank top struggles to keep her lady business where it's supposed to be.

"Hi, there, fella. You're cute in a sexy gramps kind of way," she shouts, running her hand down my arm.

"And you're kind of drunk. Don't you think it's a little early to be drinking?"

"Whoops! I think I forgot to go to bed. I'm getting married

today," she slurs, holding her hand out to show me the massive diamond ring on her finger.

"Good luck with that."

I swivel my chair further from her. I don't have time to waste talking to a drunken soon-to-be bride. I slide two crisp one hundred dollar bills into my machine, and I'm ready to win. The max bet is ten dollars a spin. You know what they say, go big or go home. The first two spins yield a big fat nothing. No worries, I'm just warming up. The machine lights up when the wheels stop on my next spin. The bells sound like a fire truck racing to a four-alarm fire.

"YOU WON!" the drunken bride-to-be shouts. "He won fifty dollars on your machine! I told you not to leave me!" She yells to one of her drunk friends who crowd around my machine.

They hoot and holler, high-fiving each other as if they won too. One kisses my cheek and asks if she can sit on my lap to take a selfie. What in the world is a selfie? I decline. Even though my machine is hot, their perfume makes my stomach churn. I need to move. They are wasting my time. The young folks usually don't play the older machines, so I head to the other side of the casino for some peace and quiet.

No less than ten minutes later, I hear a shrill voice.

"Hey, sugar, I found you!" The bride-to-be plops down in an empty chair next to mine.

"I see that," I grimace and check my watch—a little over an hour before I need to pick up Martha. I'm down seventy-five dollars—time to find another hot machine and fast.

"Leaving me again?" she whines.

"Don't you need to shower or put on a dress or something?"

"I'm not sure. Do you think I should?" She gazes at me with

glassy eyes.

I sigh and ask, "Did you want to yesterday?"

She twists her ring around her finger. "I think so."

"Maybe you shouldn't drink so much. It clouds your thoughts."

"Are you married?" she asks.

"Sure am. It was the best decision of my life. I won an amazing wife, and we built a loving family. I've been happily married for over forty years," I tell her proudly.

"Were you nervous on your wedding day?"

I imagine my young self with my beautiful Martha by my side.

"I was scared to death," I admit. "I thought about running away, but I wanted a life partner. Martha is the best partner I could ever wish for. She's smart, beautiful, and doesn't have a mean bone in her body. I'd be an idiot if I let her get away. Think of it this way— marriage is like gambling—if you don't play, you can't win. Maybe eat some food and shower before making rash decisions."

"Thank you." She smiles. The first genuine smile I've seen since I met her.

I must have said the right thing because she hugs me and walks away. Free at last. With Martha fresh in my mind, I am more determined than ever to win so I can fix the car and get her the best faucet money can buy.

Scanning the room, I see the perfect machine in a corner. It's time to get back on track. Max bets all the way. This machine is hot, and in no time, I am ahead. When I look at my watch, I do a double take. Time flies when I'm winning. I need to get out of here to pick Martha up. I slid my voucher into the cash-out machine to receive my winnings. Two hundred seventy-eight dollars. Nice. I'll come back when Martha is at her painting class. What do I have to lose?

The bills aren't due for another week or so. Plenty of time to double the money in my wallet.

The clock on my car dash tells me I need to hurry. Hopefully, I can time the lights right and reach Martha on time, so she won't ask questions about where I've been. The odds are in my favor, and I'm making good time until I nearly rear-end an old pickup. The damn truck is going twenty miles under the speed limit in a no-passing zone.

At the next light, I take a shortcut. Whipping around the corner, maybe a touch too fast, my body jerks when the tire hits the curb. A loud pop followed by violent shaking causes me to glide to a stop on the shoulder. I jump out to inspect the damage. The tire is in shreds. Thank goodness I have a spare.

I quickly loosen all the lug nuts except for one. It won't budge. Sweat burns my eyes as I search the glove box for the number to AAA. The card is at the bottom of a pile of old insurance papers. I grab my phone and push the power button—nothing. My phone won't power on, and I realize I forgot to charge it last night. Crap. I'm already late to pick up Martha, and now I can't contact her. As I pace next to the car, pondering my next move, I hear a familiar voice.

"Hey, bro. I thought that might be you, so I had my buddy turn around. Looks like you need some help."

I whip my head around and can't believe my eyes. The kid from the hardware store is sitting in the passenger seat of a truck, staring at me. Is he following me?

His friend waves from the driver's seat and yells, "Good afternoon, sir."

The kid grabs a few things from the truck. Before I can say anything, he loosens the lug nut and has the spare on and secured.

He throws the old tire in the trunk and wipes his hands on his ripped-up jeans.

"I took your advice about that girl and left her alone. You were right; hell hath no fury and shit." He hands me his phone and shakes his head. "See what she did to the car of the unlucky sucker who tried to hit it and quit it. So glad that's not my ride."

The photo shows a car covered in profanities, written with bright pink spray paint, and every window is smashed. Maybe the kid isn't as dumb as I thought.

"Thanks for the help. Sorry, I was a bit of a grump the other day," I say, handing the phone back.

"No worries. My gramps was grumpy sometimes too. Did I mention you remind me of my gramps? You would have really liked him before the dementia. I sure did."

I take out my wallet and hand him a twenty. It's the least I can do.

64

Martha

Class is over, and Walter hasn't shown up. I sit on the same bench I sat on earlier to wait for him. When Titus comes out of the building, he asks if I want some company. I can't stand him thinking he's obligated to babysit me, so I politely decline. It is not like Walter to be this late, and his phone goes straight to voicemail. The battery must be dead again. I should have asked what he was doing today, but I didn't want to listen to him drone on about his latest project. Finally, I spot him rounding the corner into the parking lot. The car is lopsided.

I hurry over and notice the spare tire. "Oh my goodness, Walter! Are you okay?" I ask, opening my door.

"I'm okay. The tire blew out after leaving the hardware store. I almost had to call AAA because of rusted lug nuts. The nice young man from the hardware store had a special tool and loosened it."

"You should have called. I was worried sick."

"My phone is dead. I'm sorry I worried you."

"Do you think the shop can repair the tire? Or will we need a new one?"

"There is no repairing that tire. When I take the car into the shop on Monday, I'll ask about new tires," he assures me.

"We have had a lot of expenses this month. Can we afford all of them?" I ask.

"It is my job to take care of you and all our expenses. Don't you worry—I got it covered," Walter says, lovingly patting my hand.

"Don't go robbing a bank or anything," I joke.

He pulls into the driveway, and I am reminded how lucky we are to have each other and our comfortable home. Walter retreats to our bedroom for a nap, so I text Bonnie to see if she's up for a walk. Within seconds, I have her reply—YES.

We meet in the middle and make loops around the neighborhood while we talk about the new reality show, *Who's Your Daddy?* Young people adopted at birth live in a house and try to figure out which older man is their biological daddy. None of the contestants seem to notice it's as easy as looking in the mirror to figure out who their daddy is. With the constant heavy drinking, it's a wonder they can complete the over-the-top challenges created to assist them in figuring out who their daddy is.

Bonnie belts out the theme song, and I laugh so hard I have to cross my legs and sit on my neighbor's lawn. As I get back up, a taxi pulls into Ashley's driveway, and Dave gets out. We watch the scene unfold as Ashley and Charlie run up to him like he's a soldier returning from war. He hands Ashley a giant bouquet and little Charlie a red fire truck.

"I can't believe the asshole is back," Bonnie huffs, her eyes narrowing.

"Maybe it will be better this time," I say, trying to sound optimistic.

"Maybe. Or maybe ol' Dave will make toast in the bathtub," Bonnie chuckles, glaring at him.

I giggle nervously, not sure she is joking. "I will tell Walter. He'll alert the neighborhood watch team. We will all keep an eye on them," I assure her.

"Thank you. What would I do without you?" Bonnie touches my arm.

We meander back to my house, where she hugs me and promises to text later. I watch her walk away, wishing I could do more to help.

65

Walter

The amber alert blares through my phone, waking me from my nap. The details are—a black 1957 Corvette, a fifteen-year-old female named Hailey, missing twenty-four hours. I race down the stairs and turn on the news to see if there is more information. A news camera pans the home where she lives with her parents, and I do a double take. It's my neighborhood. An image of young Hailey fills the screen. She looks sweet and innocent. Her parents must be worried sick.

I need more information, so I flip on my trusty police scanner. Finally, here is some info I can use. Hailey allegedly met up with a twenty-two-year-old male who she met on social media. He better not hurt her. The scanner announces the hotels the police have searched. I run to the desk to grab my old city map and quickly formulate my plan. It's up to me to find Hailey alive and unharmed.

Martha makes me eat dinner before I leave. She tells me Dave's back, and I assure her the neighborhood watch team is keeping a close eye on him. I scarf down my salad and give Martha a peck on the cheek. Driving on the spare is risky, but when a child's life is on the line, it's a risk I am willing to take.

There's not a single Corvette, let alone a vintage one, at the Red Roof Inn, Super 8, or Holiday Inn Express. I'm about to head to the Walmart parking lot when my police scanner informs me the girl has been found safe at a friend's house. The creep she was with apparently didn't realize she was a minor. What an idiot. Well, I'm glad she is safe, nonetheless.

Martha won't be expecting me home for several hours. I would be willing to bet a hundred dollars she's watching one of her boring reality shows that I have no interest in. The casino is only a few miles from here. It would be stupid not to stop in. I bet I can double the money in my wallet. Then I'll have enough to pay for the new tires and fix the air conditioning. With this plan, there won't be any need to touch the money in Martha's bank account.

I find a parking space near one of the side doors and snap a photo of the number marker. I want to avoid wandering the parking lot in the dark with all my winnings.

I head straight to the blackjack tables and find a seat at a ten-dollar minimum bet table. The seat next to mine is empty. Hopefully, I can get in a few hands before some yahoo sits down and takes the cards that should have been mine. I slide a one hundred dollar bill across the table to the dealer. A lucky current is in the air; I can feel it in my bones. My bad hip reverberates with the positive energy. Four hands later, I'm thirty dollars up. I feel phenomenal.

A young man, who doesn't look old enough to drive, plops down in an empty chair next to me. Seriously? Maybe I should cash out now. But I was taught not to leave a hot table. It's bad luck. So I stay put. A half-hour later, I have one measly ten-dollar chip. Why didn't I leave this unlucky table sooner? That immature idiot took all my good cards.

My head is pounding, and my hip throbs from sitting in the uncomfortable chair. My lonely chip and I head to the roulette table. I slide it to black. Double or nothing. The dealer spins the wheel and throws in the small white ball. The ball spins for what seems like ages and finally lands on red. What the hell? Just like that, it's over. Or is it? No way am I going to leave on a low note. I pull out another hundred from my wallet. The dealer slides over a pile of chips, and I place them all on black. My brain spins right along with that little white ball. As the wheel slows, the ball bounces into a black space, and I suck in a deep breath. At the last second, I watch the little ball jump to the red space next to where it initially landed. No way! It looks to me like a drunk idiot bumped the table.

When I yell my complaint to the dealer, he says, "Relax, old timer," in a condescending tone. He doesn't even care. He's probably in cahoots with the casino. They should be ashamed of themselves for stealing the older generation's money like that.

My only choice now is to get home to Martha before she starts worrying. If I transfer some money from Martha's account into our joint account, I can come back later this week to win my money back. During the day, there won't be as many drunk idiots messing up my games. The funds will be back in Martha's account before she realizes I borrowed a little.

At least the entire night wasn't a bust. I helped bring that girl home safely. On the drive home, I keep my speed at forty-nine miles per hour. I wouldn't want to be reckless.

66

Journal

Don't get me started on that no-good pile of crap being back and acting all nice. My mama always said you could take a piece of poo and wrap it up in a fancy box with a silver bow, but it's still gonna stink.

Now that the teenage hussy is back where she belongs, I got all the time in the world to keep my eyes on ol' Dave. I walk the neighborhood loop, giving Dave the evil eye every time I pass his house. He knows I'm watching him, and he better watch his back.

My know it all therapist would say, "The best way to deal with pent-up energy is by being active, plus it will help you sleep." The only way I'll sleep better is when that good-for-nothing is locked up where he belongs. Or better yet, when he's sleeping in a pine box six feet underground.

67

Walter

By the time I get home, Martha is already upstairs, tucked into bed, reading one of her thick novels. She mentions that I smell like an ashtray. I need to remember to put air freshener spray in the car. I tell her I didn't leave any stone unturned in my search for the missing girl, including checking out a few smoky dive bars. She seems satisfied with my response and goes back to reading her book. I'm hoping she will be sound asleep after I shower so that I can take care of business.

She's still reading when I crawl into bed, so I grab my true crime book and stare at the pages, hoping she gets tired soon. Finally, she marks her page with a bookmark and turns out her bedside lamp. After a quick goodnight kiss, I turn out my light and listen for her heavy breathing. When I'm positive she's asleep, I tiptoe to Martha's nightstand and take her cell phone. I sneak downstairs to the kitchen, where the laptop sits on the table. I'm thankful we keep a small notebook with all our account information, just in case one of us dies unexpectedly. I flip through the notebook and then carefully enter her account information into the bank website. I'm in.

First, I adjust the notifications to go to my cell phone instead of hers. Thank God I took that computer class down at the library. Her cell chimes with a security code, and I enter that onto the bank site and then delete the message. Next, I sign up for paperless delivery of statements and make sure they are going to my email. A chime on the laptop alerts me that the bank sent an email notifying her of the changes. I transfer a thousand dollars from her account to our joint account. There will be plenty to pay for the car repairs and tires, with some left over for the casino, where I will win back every dime. Lastly, I check the emails on her phone and the computer to ensure the bank notifications are all deleted—no sense in worrying Martha. I finally climb into bed, knowing I'll be out like a light when my head hits that pillow. All this banking and police work makes me feel like I'm back at work.

68

Martha

Even though it's Sunday, I'm up early. There's no rest for the weary. I have so much cleaning to do. The house has suffered with all my extracurricular activities. You would be surprised by how much filth two people can generate. Or maybe I should say one person. This house would be as neat as a pin if I were the only person living here.

First, I throw the bathroom rugs into the washing machine. While the washer does its magic, I mop the kitchen, dust the living room, and change the kitty litter. Walter finally moseys downstairs as I sit down for a cup of coffee.

"What are you doing today?" he asks, pouring himself a cup.

It takes everything in me not to roll my eyes or scream. Is he kidding? The house smells like fresh lemon, for Pete's sake.

The thought of ignoring him did cross my mind, but my daddy always said, "In the end, kindness is what matters." I sure do miss my daddy.

Instead, I take a sip of coffee and answer, "The cleaning."

"Need any help?" he asks.

I take a deep breath. Walter possesses many talents; handyman, car maintenance, and paying the bills. However, cleaning is not one of the skills that come naturally to him. Over the years, I have had to re-clean hundreds of things he thought he had cleaned.

"Thanks for the offer, but you have been so busy lately. Why don't you take the day off?" I suggest.

He takes a leftover piece of the quiche I made for dinner a couple of days ago out to the front porch. At least he's not in here messing up what I already cleaned. My break is over; I get back to work. Walter disrupts my thoughts when he comes inside. I watch as he puts his dirty dish in the sink adjacent to the empty dishwasher.

"Are you sure I can't help with anything?" he shouts over the hum of the vacuum.

I shake my head no. "It's my joy to take care of you. Go relax."

69

Walter

Martha is up early cleaning. She cleans as if *Better Homes and Gardens* is showing up for a photo shoot. If our home is not spotless, she is stressed. Can you imagine being worried about a little mess? I wish that were my only problem. She doesn't take me up on my offer to help, but later she'll complain she had to do all the work alone. At least I know what's coming. It is comforting to know her so well. The best thing to do when she is in a cleaning mood is to stay out of her way. It's a lovely morning for breakfast and a little light reading on the front porch. I'm just getting to the good part of the memoir I'm reading about the man who caught the Golden State Killer. I hope to write a book like this one day, passing on my skills to the next generation.

After I take care of my dirty dish, I decide to run to the store to get something to grill later. Martha won't let me help clean, so I will handle dinner and let her take the afternoon off. I love taking care of my favorite girl.

70

Martha

Walter is driving me crazy with his constant pestering, and I am thankful when my phone pings to an incoming text from Bonnie.

Trevor hurt his ankle. Can't golf for six weeks. Going crazy already.

I understand!

And I'm so stressed with that asshole being back. I swear if Dave lays another hand on my daughter or Charlie, I will kill him.

I barely have time to read her text when another comes in.

Not really kill him, hahaha. Just a figure of speech— government who is always watching.

Another text from Bonnie.

But I might murder him.

And then another.

Not really murder, government, maybe yell at loudly and kick in the crotch.

I literally laugh out loud and send a text back.

I totally understand! Walter alerted the neighborhood watch. We are all keeping an eye on him. Want to join me on a hike? You will have to drive. Walter got a flat, and I don't trust the spare.

As the second's tick by with no response, I regret my decision to ask. Bonnie is probably too stressed out. Finally—my phone pings.

I would love that! I can be at your house in 15 minutes

Perfect, I will be ready—smiling face emoji.

I am waiting on the front porch when Bonnie pulls up. I jump in her car, placing two water bottles in the cupholders. She appreciates the gesture and tells me she didn't even think of bringing a water bottle with everything on her mind. I navigate us to one of my favorite hiking spots. Walter and I loved these mountain trails in our younger days. We would hike this park with the boys at least once a month. The cliff's stunning views are spectacular.

The trails are as beautiful as I remember. The weather is warm, but several big, white, fluffy clouds block some of the sun's rays. A low fence protects my favorite lookout spot. I carefully climb over the fence and shuffle closer to the cliff's edge. I'm not a fan of heights, but the view is much better on the ledge. Bonnie waltzes right up to the edge and peers down the cliff to the bottom. I grab a low-hanging branch of one of the old pines and hold onto Bonnie's flowing shirt with my other hand.

"Am I making you nervous?" She grins at me when she realizes I'm gripping her shirt.

I laugh and let go. "It's the mom in me. Always trying to keep everyone safe."

She takes a couple of steps back, and I breathe a sigh of relief. We stand in silence for several minutes, taking in the view.

"It is truly stunning," Bonnie whispers.

I nod my head in agreement.

"Thank you for inviting me today." Bonnie smiles at me. "Being out in nature is exactly what I needed. You are such a good friend Martha."

Bonnie wraps her arm around my shoulder for a quick hug. My heart swells with happiness as I return the gesture.

I had forgotten how much I loved this trail. I promise to make it a point to come back, even if it is on my own.

71

Walter

I walk to the store because I can't risk driving on the spare again. My day brightens when I see Fran working the lotto counter. She usually doesn't work on Sundays. It would be a shame not to say hello, and as long as I'm over there, I might as well grab a few scratchers. Today is shaping up to be a lucky day.

"Fancy seeing you here on Sunday. Thought you had Sundays off?" I ask.

She greets me with a warm smile. "How observant of you. The young lady who works Sundays had family issues, so I'm helping out." Fran lowers her voice and continues, "I don't like to gossip, but I think her husband is abusive. No matter the heat, she wears long sleeves to cover her bruises." Fran shakes her head and lowers her voice even further, "She told me how her son broke his arm. I did not believe a word of it. You do a lot with the police force, right? Is there anything I should be doing?" Fran asks.

"You can report it to the police. You will need proof, or they won't do much. Especially if she hasn't pressed charges."

"The situation makes me so angry. Ashley is the sweetest

woman you could ever meet. I want to strangle that man for hurting her and that sweet boy," Fran says through gritted teeth.

"Don't do that. I would hate to see you in an orange jumpsuit on the news," I say, patting her hand.

"I guess you're right. Orange is not my color." She shrugs. "How many tickets do you want today, sugar?"

I pull out my last twenty. "How about four of the five-dollar winners? You pick."

"Coming right up."

I tuck the tickets in my wallet—time to get the groceries. I'll scratch them when I have time to concentrate on winning. Martha requested fish. I hope I can find a fish that tastes like steak.

72

Fran

Lotto sales are slow on Sundays. It must be all those people trying to do right by God at least once a week. The church was never my thing. Once I knew the good Lord made me the way I am, I knew the Catholic church I grew up in wasn't for me.

The only reason I would rather be home is to keep an eye on Ashley's house. With her asshole husband back, I keep my windows open a crack so I can hear if she yells for help. She probably doesn't even realize we live right down the street from her. We recently moved to the neighborhood to be closer to the store. Susan was tired of driving thirty minutes across town whenever a cashier called in sick, or a stocker saw a tiny rat. I planned to let Ashley know we are neighbors until I overheard her tell a coworker that her parents live in her neighborhood and she has no privacy. After hearing that, I was reluctant to tell Ashley that Susan and I lived two doors down from her. Susan figured that after the summer heat, we would be outside working, and we could run into each other and pretend we didn't know she lived there.

Our shady front porch is one of my favorite places to read. I always have one ear tuned in just in case there's trouble. I walk our golden retrievers, Laker and Peanut, past Ashley's house every night after sunset to guarantee she is safe. It breaks my heart that she feels stuck with that good-for-nothing.

My therapist once told me I was too emotional. Well, I think some people aren't emotional enough. Maybe I wouldn't have to care so much if others cared, even a little.

73

Journal

My lazy therapist once told me, "Make sure you relax and take care of yourself." After all the work I've been doing lately, I did deserve to relax a little bit. And what better way than on the front porch with a book and my sweet tea?

As I cracked open my book, an elderly man wandered up my driveway and walked up my porch steps. Before I could say anything, he plopped down right next to me on my swing. The first thing that hit me was his stench. He smelled bad enough to gag a maggot. My stomach protested, and I thought I would lose my breakfast. I jumped out of the swing and took a good look at him. His cornbread wasn't even close to being done in the middle. His shirt was buttoned up all wrong, and he wore a slipper on one foot and only a sock on the other.

He started screaming that it was time for school. I calmly told him it was Sunday, and there was no school on Sunday. He started yelling about how mad his ma would be if he didn't get to school. This guy was as confused as a fart in a fan factory. I told him his ma ain't here, so she can't be mad, and he better get off my property. Don't judge me. You would have done the same thing if you were in my shoes.

He stared at me just like my granny used to when she lost her mind. I knew right then and there what I was dealing with. That's when he started yelling for candy. The only candy I could find was an old bag of Halloween suckers. They would have to do. Before I handed him the sucker, I made him promise to leave. Wouldn't you know it, he agreed, so I gave him the sucker. You'll never believe what happened next. He grabbed it, looked at it, and whipped it into my yard. He said he didn't want a sucker. He wanted a candy bar. I done near lost it. Even if I had a candy bar, there's no way I would give him one.

He crossed his arms and pouted, so I pretended to read, hoping he would get bored and leave. He kept repeating "candy bar" over and over, and I couldn't take it anymore. I went into a full hissy fit and told him to get off my porch. And I may have gone and lost my mind because I told him he was a bad boy and his ma was going to be madder than a wet hen. Now mind you, I'm not proud of how I was acting. I know he can't help his mind being scrambled and all, but what was I supposed to do? If I were in charge of his care, I would be smart enough to keep him from stinking like poo and roaming the neighborhood.

I was pondering my next move when a lady walked up my porch steps. She grabbed the old man's hand and had the nerve to ask me what I had done. Can you believe that? I was trying to be helpful. She asked him why he was upset, and he said I told him his ma would be mad because he was a naughty boy. The expression on her face was pure disgust. She started pulling him off my porch and shouted that her daddy has Alzheimer's, and I should be ashamed of myself. She's the one who should be ashamed of herself. Can't even keep tabs on her old man. No words came to my mouth because I was in shock. The only good news was she took her old man with her when she left. The old fart picked up the sucker from the lawn and said, "I'll see you tomorrow." The nerve.

74

Martha

The sun isn't even awake when I start digging through my closet. I need something special to wear to my painting class. A summer blouse (from the 1980s) hangs in the back of my closet. It still fits and looks pretty good in a vintage, bohemian way, and reminds me of something Bonnie would wear. A pair of capris and my new ring complete the outfit. A final glance in the mirror reveals the ring is a bit much for painting class, so I return it to my jewelry box.

In the kitchen, Walter is waiting for me. He has already made the coffee. He must be excited to get the car fixed.

"I haven't seen that top in twenty years. If I recall, we had a lot of fun times when you wore that shirt," he says with a sly smile.

"Thanks. It's so old I won't have to worry about getting paint on it." I shrug and take a sip of my coffee.

75

Walter

Martha was in a mood this morning and not the good kind. As soon as she leaves, I pull the scratchers I bought yesterday out of my wallet. I start scratching while I finish my coffee. Every single one is defective. Damn it. I hope this isn't foreshadowing as to what this day is going to be like. I better get to the bank and withdraw the money I need to fix the car.

My favorite cashier, Olivia, handles the transaction. "Doing anything fun today?" she inquires.

"Just boring car repairs." My mind isn't coming up with anything witty to say.

She counts out my money two times (another reason she's my favorite) and places seven hundred dollars in an envelope.

"Can I make you a cup of coffee for your journey?" she asks with a smile.

"Sure. That would hit the spot," I reply, returning a smile.

"French vanilla, original, or hazelnut?" Olivia asks as I follow her to the complimentary coffee station.

"French vanilla. Merci," I say in my best French accent.

She giggles at my joke and tells me she hopes I have a good day. My luck is already turning around.

I buzz by the senior center to get a free donut with my free coffee. Only four donut holes left. I pop them in my mouth, one after the other, and throw away the empty box. Martha would be proud I'm cleaning up after myself.

After the mechanic checks the car in, I make myself at home in the waiting area. The magazines are from three years ago, but it doesn't matter. The only thing I am concentrating on is the clock on the wall. A half-hour passes with no word from the mechanic. My car is being held hostage.

Finally, the mechanic calls me up to the counter. I am not surprised when he tells me the bad news. The air conditioner has a crack and will cost five hundred and thirty dollars to fix. On top of the three hundred eighty dollars for two new tires. Thank goodness he offers a loaner car. I need to run home to transfer more money to cover this fiasco.

The house is quiet, and I am again grateful that Martha has picked up some interests. I open the laptop and go right to the bank account. Another thousand should be plenty for now. I cover my tracks and delete the email that follows the transaction. Next stop—the bank.

"Twice in one day? What a treat," Olivia greets me.

"My money brings me in, but the customer service brings me back." Finally, I came up with something witty to say.

"Deposit or withdrawal this time?" she asks.

"Unfortunately, withdrawal. The car repairs are a bit more than I previously thought they would be," I grimace. "I'm going to need another eight hundred bucks."

"Well, that is a bummer. Will a sucker make it better?" Olivia asks sweetly.

"It will help," I tell her as she hands me a cherry sucker, my favorite.

She knows me well. I pop the sucker into my mouth and stroll out of the bank. There is no way I'm going back to watch the clock tick by slowly in the car repair waiting room. By my calculations, this job will take hours. I might as well go to the casino and earn back the money I need. As luck would have it, my favorite spot near the side door is available.

76

Martha

The instructor is the only person at the park when I arrive for class. She is once again having difficulty setting up. When I offer assistance, her face fills with relief. Moments later, Bonnie comes and jumps in to help.

"Love your top! Where did you get it?" Bonnie asks.

"1983," I laugh.

Class starts right on schedule, thanks to our help. Our instructor gives a quick tutorial on today's subject matter, and then we get to work.

"How is Trevor?" I ask.

"He is driving me crazy," Bonnie sighs. "I'm starting to feel like his personal maid. 'Can I have a snack?' 'Can you reach the remote?'" she imitates Trevor's deep voice. "All he watches on TV are old westerns. If I hear another gun shootout, I'm going to scream. But I put on a happy face and pretend it isn't making me crazy. Listen to me. I've become a bitter old lady." Bonnie laughs. "How are you?"

"I totally understand. I've gotten good at pretending Walter isn't driving me nuts when he follows me around the house like a lost puppy. I seriously might lose my mind if I hear his police scanner blare one more time." I lower my voice before saying, "Yesterday, I was praying for someone to get murdered to get him out of the house. I'm a terrible person, right?"

Bonnie laughs and whispers, "No worse than me. Don't tell anyone, but I used to pray that Trevor would develop a medical problem. I didn't want him to die. Just something minor where he would have to stay at the hospital for a couple of weeks for testing or observation. I needed a break badly." We laugh together.

Having a friend with whom I can be my true self and who understands me is refreshing.

77

Walter

No time for slots today. I need to win big money fast. I take four hundred dollars from my wallet and push the bills across the high-limit poker table. The dealer is a beautiful blond. Money vibes radiate from her as she slides several stacks of chips in front of me. Even her fingernails have dollar signs on them. A glance around the table tells me none of the other players are as smart as me. This is the perfect spot to be the winner.

The attractive dealer winks at me whenever I win a hand, and I can't help smiling. She is my silent partner in our quest to win big. I tip her after all my big wins, so she will keep the good cards coming my way. The poor woman to my right gets up and leaves after I take all her money. A smart-looking man wearing a suit and tie takes the empty seat. He doesn't have a hair out of place. I'm sure he will be harder to beat, but I'm up for the challenge. After all, I'm on a roll and have my lucky charm dealer passing me all the good cards. As the new player gets settled, an elderly gentleman replaces the dealer. She wishes us the best of luck, staring at me when she speaks. For a split second I also think about leaving, but decide to stay. I can quickly pay all my bills when I win the dapper player's money.

The next hand is a nail-biter. The suave man is all in. I have a winning hand, so I also decide to go all in. The other players fold, as they should. I flip my cards over, showing a full house—ten high. The handsome young man smirks and reveals a full house—queens high. The other players gasp as I sink into my chair. My forehead breaks out in a cold sweat, and my lips tingle. I take a deep breath to regain my composure and shake the young man's hand. The game was exhilarating, even with the loss. It was an honor to play with a man as skilled as myself. I needed a break from poker anyway. My heart can't take more right now.

I check my phone to see a text from the mechanic. My car is ready. I need a big win fast. Walking to the roulette table, I take a hundred dollar bill out of my wallet. When the dealer asks if I want five-dollar chips, I shake my head and tell him to give me a hundred dollar chip. It's all going on black. The gray-haired gentleman to my left glances at me and slides several more of his chips to black. He knows luck when he sees it. And there are no drunk idiots to mess up my chances this time. The tiny white ball spins for ages before finally resting on black, just as I knew it would. I doubled my money—time to cash out my winnings. The cute cashier slides two crisp one hundred dollar bills through the slot. Not bad for a couple of hours.

78

Journal

I can't stop thinking about how that lady yelled at me. That's what I get for trying to help. Everyone knows I'm a good person. And it certainly is not my fault she can't keep tabs on her daddy.

Never mind. I took the initiative and did a little research on the google wikiHow page to learn all about Alzheimer's. I was going to be prepared if a certain someone showed up again.

You might be asking, "Is it worth it? If you stayed inside, you wouldn't have anything to worry about." Let's get one thing straight right here and now. I will not be held hostage by an old man. Plus, I needed to be outside protecting the neighborhood. Sitting in my house and only caring about myself is selfish. Everyone knows that's not like me. I will be planted right on my front porch with my latest book. It's a real page-turner. I usually have these kinds of books solved within the first three chapters but not this one. There have been so many twists and turns, and everyone has it out for the sick bastard who ended up pushing up daisies. I only had eighty-five pages left, and I still didn't have one iota who did it.

So there I was, minding my own business, about to solve the mystery, when guess who showed up? I know, I know, I should have been watching. But I was lost in my story, and he appeared out of nowhere. Only one button on his shirt was buttoned, and his belly was hanging in the wind. No one wants to see that. And he smelled like that time the sewer backed up in the basement.

He asked me if I wanted to play a game. I told him not today in my calmest voice, exactly like wikiHow told me to. I asked him who he was planning to visit next. An excellent open-ended question. He told me he was going to stay with me. I told him no, siree. I'm busy reading and prefer it nice and peaceful when I read. He kept insisting his ma told him to come to my house so I could keep an eye on him. It didn't matter a lick as to what I said because his mind would never make sense of it. He just kept repeating the same thing.

I decided my best plan would be to ignore him. I picked up my book and pretended to read. You'll never guess what the old fart said next! He wanted to play hide-n-seek and started walking to my front door. I yelled "NO" and grabbed my door handle faster than a one-legged man in a butt-kicking contest. I hung on for dear life. No way was I going to let him in my house! He had the nerve to push me. He may be old, but he has arms of steel. I used every ounce of my strength to keep that door closed. The next time he tried, I was ready. I let go with one hand and pushed my palm right into his face. And wouldn't you know it, the blood started flowing like the Nile River, and he started screaming bloody murder.

Before I could do anything, that same young woman came strutting from over yonder. She started screaming that she saw me punch her daddy with her own two eyes. I tried explaining that he was trying to break into my house. She had the nerve to say he probably needed the bathroom and I shouldn't punch people. You are never going to believe what happened next. She threatened to call the police.

Not today, Satan. No way was I going to stand by and let her threaten me on my property. I told her that maybe I should call Adult Protective Services because she clearly couldn't care for her daddy. I told her she should be ashamed of herself for letting him walk around in filth with no one watching him while he went who knows where doing who knows what.

She had the nerve to say she takes good care of her daddy. Never you mind, though. I got the last word when I yelled, "Doesn't smell like it," as she dragged him down my driveway.

I tried reading my book, but I couldn't concentrate. That incompetent woman's words looped in my mind. She better think twice before she goes calling the authorities. Two can play that game, and ain't nobody better at game playing than me.

79

Martha

Walter woke up on the wrong side of the bed, and for some reason, he thinks I should join in on the misery. Every time I try to make conversation to get to the bottom of his lousy mood, he snaps at me. The last time Walter acted like this was when our financial situation was grim. That memory makes me worry. He finally decides to take a drive to test the air conditioning in the car. I breathe a sigh of relief when he leaves.

As soon as the car rounds the corner, I grab the laptop and go to the bank's website. I attempt to log in, but a message says my password is incorrect. I try again with the same result. After making sure the caps lock is off, I try one more time, typing each letter one at a time. I am confident I entered the password correctly this time. Nope—wrong again. A message alerts me that my account is locked due to numerous failed attempts. If I call the bank to reset the password, I will need to tell Walter. He'll be upset that I didn't trust him and frustrated because he will have to remember a new password. It's best to pretend it didn't happen, so I close the laptop. If he asks, I will tell him the truth. If he doesn't, he doesn't need to know. With the mood he's been in, why start a fight? After all the trouble we had with his gambling, I'm confident he would never do that again. He wouldn't jeopardize our relationship. I need to quit worrying all the time and enjoy my life. Maybe I will mix up some of his favorite cookies and eat a few while I watch *Who's Your Daddy?*

80

Walter

The car's air conditioning smacks me in the face when the car rumbles to life. I'm glad it works. For the money I spent, it better. As long as I have the car, I might as well hit the casino. Martha was so cranky; maybe I'll eat dinner there too. I love my wife with all my heart, but some days we need a little time apart. Whoever said, "Absence makes the heart grow fonder," knew what they were talking about.

For a Tuesday, the casino is hopping. They must be having one of their giveaways again. The damn giveaways bring crowds, and I don't like crowds. I have to park out in the back lot.

Since none of my favorite slot machines are available, I decide it's a good day to do a little sports betting while I enjoy a beer. A perfect spot is open at the bar. I can watch five TVs, and a bowl of pretzels is within my reach. My luck is already improving. The bartender appears too young to have a job. However, he quickly proves himself when he serves me an ice-cold beer less than two minutes after I sit down. I also order the nachos with all the fixings and settle in to figure out which games to bet on. Three beers in, I am up over five hundred dollars. Not bad. Glancing at my watch, I realize I have been sitting here for hours. I better get home before I'm too drunk to drive, or worse, Martha starts to worry.

The soaring afternoon temperatures make my car feel like a furnace. I crank the air and hit the road, racking my brain for an excuse as to why I smell like smoke. Maybe I stopped to help put out a fire. Better make that a barn fire. If I say it was a house fire, Martha will get online to look up the victims, hoping one of them is the same size as her so she can unload some old clothes on them. She will make them her famous mac and cheese and walk up to what used to be their porch with her treasures in hand. Nope, not going to make that mistake again. Flipping my police scanner on, I hope for an actual fire. I must have used all my good luck at the casino because there are no barn fires. Thank goodness Martha will be none the wiser with my scanner in the car.

When I get home, Martha is sleeping. She must not be feeling well because she never sleeps in the afternoon—says it ruins a good night's sleep. This is the perfect opportunity to shower, so I won't have to lie to Martha about a fire. First, I put my winnings in an envelope in the desk drawer. It would be plain dumb to carry this much cash around. I keep one hundred in my wallet—for an emergency. The phone rings as I'm headed up the stairs to the bathroom. I quickly grab it so it won't wake Martha. Frank's deafening voice comes through the other end. I missed my community watch shift. Damn it; I knew I was supposed to do something other than win big at the casino today.

"Are you sure? I thought I was on for tomorrow," I lie. I know he's right, but I will never admit that to Frank.

"I am certain. Do you want to take my afternoon shift instead?" Frank screams so loudly my ears are ringing.

"Sure, I can do that. Let me go and get changed."

I hurry upstairs to grab my uniform. My sweet Martha pressed it for me. After a quick shower, I am ready to serve. Before making my rounds, I send Martha a text message to let her know where I am.

Not a darn thing is happening in our neighborhood. I know I should be happy to live in a nice area, but living in a crime-free community is boring when your only job is to control crime. I bet the community officers in New York and Los Angeles never drive around for hours with nothing to do. Honestly, the only place I want to be right now is at the casino.

81

Martha

The chime on my phone startles me awake—a text message from Walter. He is working the afternoon shift for the community watch task force. That means three more hours, all to myself. Maybe more if he discovers a crime and needs to investigate.

Fluffing my pillow, I try to go back to sleep but can't. Walter's text message ruined the moment. There's no sense of staying in bed all day, so I decide to freshen up. The bathroom smells like a dirty ashtray—time for a little investigating of my own. Walter's crumpled shirt is next to the hamper. So close, yet so far. I hold it to my nose and almost gag from the stench. Are you kidding me? Fine, let him take up smoking in his old age. Good luck to him. I won't feel sorry for him when he's battling lung cancer. He better not smoke in the house or the car, though, then he will have a real problem. Me.

I throw the shirt in the hamper and spray the air freshener. While I freshen up, I remember how Walter smelled when sneaking around gambling at the casino. My heart feels like it might pound right out of my chest. Could he be gambling again? There's one way to find out. I race down the stairs to the desk and yank open drawer after drawer. In my frenzy, I pull too hard, spilling the contents of an entire drawer onto the floor. I pick up the pieces, old coins from my daddy, our passports (such a waste since we never go anywhere), and the life insurance policy, but no envelope with money. My heart sinks. On my hands and knees, I search under the sofa, barely able to breathe. When I see a white envelope, a rush of air leaves my lungs. Nestled inside are four one-hundred dollar bills. He isn't gambling. No way would there be this much money left if he was. I knew he wouldn't risk our marriage again.

After I start a load of laundry, including his smelly shirt, I plop down on the couch and put my feet on the coffee table. As luck would have it, I find a *Law & Order* marathon. It's always fun getting lost in a story about a crime solved in less than sixty minutes and neatly wrapped up with a conviction and jail time for the perp.

82

Fran

Today is usually my favorite day of the week. One day neither Susan nor I have to work. We typically enjoy doing something fun together on our day off. However, I can't shake the bad vibes from the nightmare I had last night. I was selling lotto tickets to Satan. I woke up in a cold sweat and had difficulty falling back asleep. After tossing and turning for hours, I decided to get up so I wouldn't disturb Susan. I'm in the kitchen drinking my second cup of coffee when she comes downstairs. She kisses my head and then does the same to our twin golden retrievers and sweet cat.

"I must be working in hell," I say while pouring her a cup of coffee.

She looks at me quizzically, so I relay my nightmare to her.

In all seriousness, she asks, "Were his tickets winners?"

"Very funny," I reply. "And no, Satan's tickets were losers like everyone else's."

"I think if you worked in hell, Satan would only get winners, so he could keep coming back to torture you." She grins at me.

She does have a point.

We planned on relaxing on the front porch this morning, reading a book, and hanging out with our fur babies. However, focusing on my book is impossible when we settle on the porch swing. I find myself staring toward Ashley's house. I know she's safe at the moment because she's working the lotto counter at the store, but that doesn't stop me from obsessively watching her house for signs of danger. Laker senses my stress and barks whenever the wind blows as he paces, circling my feet. Finally, when Susan can't take the tension any longer, she suggests we take the dogs on a hike. I insist she should go, but I want to stay close to home today. She kisses me on the cheek before calling the dogs to the car. The cat jumps onto my lap to keep me company.

83

Martha

Different day, same Walter. All I want to do is enjoy my coffee in peace. All he wants to do is pester me with his incessant talking. As I flip through my *Good Housekeeping* magazine, he asks a question I don't hear. I give an um-hum so he won't detect my annoyance. Small tricks you learn after being married for what seems like forever. The loud, high-pitched screech comes next, and I jump up so fast that my chair tips over, landing with a heavy thud on the linoleum. The rush of my heartbeat whooshes in my ears, and I clutch my chest.

Walter asks if I'm okay and rights the chair for me to sit back down.

"Didn't you hear me?" he shouts over the relentless beeping. "I asked if I should check the smoke alarm, and you said, um-hum."

I paint a smile on my face that I trace with my fingertips, checking for a stroke. I make a mental note to ask my doctor about pain when startled and wonder if Walter would be charged with my murder if he scares me to death.

"Please stop," I beg.

"Do you want to go to the library?" he asks, not skipping a beat.

"We could both get a new book."

"No, thank you. Why don't you go? It's a beautiful day for you to take a walk." I cross my fingers, hoping he will take my suggestion.

"What time do you need me back?" he asks.

"I'm planning to have dinner ready at six," I tell him, saying a silent prayer that he takes the hint.

84

Walter

I have all the time in the world with Martha kicking me out of the house for the day. A stop at the senior center is in order. Five, almost full, boxes of donuts are open on the front table. It's going to be a good day, after all. I grab one, wrap it in a napkin, and put it in my pocket for later. I take two more, one for each hand, to eat on my walk to the store. I might as well keep my winning streak going with a few scratchers.

My neighbor, Ashley, is working the lotto counter. Despite today's eighty-five-degree temperature, she is wearing a sweater three sizes too big.

"Good afternoon. Nice to see you today," I say, trying to hide my disappointment that Fran isn't working.

"How can I help you?" she asks politely.

"How about four five-dollar scratchers? You pick the winners."

Leaning in, she whispers, "I have been paying attention to the cards people turn in, and I think I figured out the system. You can't blame me if they aren't winners, but feel free to split the money with me if you do win big," she says with a little giggle.

I've always had a way with women. It's a gift.

Ashley reaches up for the roll of tickets at the top, and her sweater slides down to her elbow. Finger marks wrap around her arm in shades of purple and orange. I stop myself from gasping, and I'm grateful she can't see my face. Ashley quickly moves the sweater back in place and hands me the tickets with a sweet smile. When I look at her face, the caked makeup hiding a bruise on her cheek is all I can see. Her swollen face reveals sad, tired eyes.

"Are you doing okay, Ashley? Martha and I are here to help if you ever need anything." My eyes lock with hers as I try to express my concern without more words.

"Thank you, Walter. Charlie loves your golf cart. He gets so excited every time you drive by." She tries to change the subject.

"Maybe I can give him a ride around the block one day," I offer.

"He would love that. I will ask his daddy if that's okay and let you know," she says, avoiding my eyes.

"Sure. Let me know."

As I walk away, I am fuming. I'm a community officer and can't protect my neighbors. I shove the tickets into my wallet and walk to the police station. Frank is sitting on the golf cart in front of the station, pestering a young officer.

"Did someone steal your car?" he yells.

I'm in no mood to deal with him today. I whip open the station door. The cadet sitting at the front counter doesn't look a day over eighteen.

"How can I help you today?" he asks in a tiny voice.

"I need to speak to an officer," I say, staring him down. "I have to file an abuse charge."

He holds my gaze and replies, "I would be happy to file a report for you. An officer will investigate your concerns as soon as possible."

"I would prefer to speak to someone now." No way am I backing down.

"I am someone. And I would be happy to file a report for you."

My blood starts to boil. A group of officers is sitting behind him, doing nothing but talking and laughing.

"Are you sure none of the other officers can help me?" I ask through gritted teeth.

"Policy, sir. I promise to give the report to the officers. We get a lot of people coming in to file claims. If we interrupted them every time someone came in, they wouldn't get any work done."

"Doesn't look like they are getting any work done right now." I nod in the direction of the chatty officers.

"I assure you they are," he insists.

I relent and explain my suspicion of abuse to him. I tap my foot as he clicks on the computer keyboard, one letter at a time. Don't they teach typing in high school anymore?

"I will have an officer contact you once they finish the investigation," he assures me with his crooked grin.

"Yup, as soon as they finish their important work, have them call me." I roll my eyes and stomp out of the station.

I might as well head to the library. My favorite author just released a new true crime book. The librarian always holds a copy of my favorites for me. I'm telling you, it's my charm. The ladies can't resist me.

85

Journal

I know what you're thinking. Stay in your house. Read on the sofa or catch a nap, for Pete's sake. Believe me, I would if I could, but someone has to keep an eye on that good-for-nothing neighbor Dave and be ready to call the authorities at any sign of trouble. If I'm all safe and secure in my house, that snake in the grass could be getting away with harming his lovely wife and sweet little boy. How would I feel if the worst happened while I was relaxing, not giving one iota about my community? No sir. Not me.

I brought out my keys and locked my front door this time. My mama didn't raise a fool. If that man, who was clearly a few fries short of a Happy Meal, came by, I would not let him get past me this time.

I had just cracked open my book when wouldn't you know it? I saw him walking up my front path, but I was ready this time and met him before he could get up the porch steps. His shirt was covered with Lord knows what, and he stunk like a hog in a steam bath.

I immediately told him that I wasn't interested in any company today. He told me that his ma told him to play at my house. Well, two can play the ma games, so I told him my ma told me I'm not allowed to have visitors. I searched up and down the street for his lazy daughter, but she done near vanished again. Caregiver, my ass. She's probably collecting money from the state while I do all the work watching him.

You'll never believe what he said next. He told me his ma said I was supposed to take him to the park today. I said sorry, I couldn't because I had a very important book report I needed to finish and held up my book to prove it. He didn't care. He kept shouting he wanted to go to the park. When I raised my voice and told him to put an egg in his shoe and beat it, he turned and started walking away. I breathed a big sigh of relief. I certainly don't have time for his shenanigans when I have important things to do, like protecting my neighborhood.

I relaxed as I watched him walk away, but the next thing I knew, he stopped and tried my car door. As I watched him climb into the passenger seat, I cursed myself for not thinking ahead and locking my car. I scanned the road one more time for his negligent caregiver. Not a soul around in either direction. The only thing I could think was how in the world this senile man, who was probably relieving his bowels in my car at this very moment, had become my problem.

Now, I'm not proud of this next part, but I had to do something, so I made a snap decision. I would take him to the park if he wanted to go to the park. Don't judge me because I know you would have done the same thing if it was you.

I got in the driver's side and slammed my door so hard the whole car shook. The car was hotter than blue blazes making his stench worse. I was about to taste my breakfast all over again, and believe me, it's not nearly as good the second time around. I rolled all the windows down and raced out of the neighborhood faster than a hot knife through butter. Thank goodness the heat was keeping the lazy folks in their homes. No way did I need someone spotting me with the old fart in my car. Let me tell you a thing or two. His daughter needed to learn a lesson the hard way.

I decided the outlet mall playground was the best place to drop him off.

The stores weren't open yet, but they would be soon enough. Someone would find him and call the police once they realized he was a Jenga game that had already collapsed.

I backed into a spot near the entrance. When he saw the playground, he jumped out of the car and slammed the door. The first thing I did was click the locks because I learned a lesson today too. By the time he looked back, I was already driving away. I shouted, "Have fun at the park!" and I really hoped he would have a great time.

86

Walter

I turn the corner into the neighborhood to see several police cars one road over from mine. That young cadet must have typed in the wrong address on my complaint. I knew I should have insisted on talking to an official officer. An older officer leans against his cruiser. His name tag says Smith. Finally, I can speak to someone with good sense.

"Good afternoon. I'm Walter, a trained community officer. Are you investigating the domestic abuse claim I filed?" I ask.

"I don't know anything about a domestic abuse claim. We are investigating a missing person case." He pulls out his phone and shows me a picture of an elderly gentleman. "His last name is Johnson."

I recognize the man. He moved in with his daughter not too long ago.

"I haven't seen him today," I inform Officer Smith.

Frank pulls up in the golf cart, wearing his community patrol officer badge, and yells, "Hi there, Kevin. How's the wife?" Frank doesn't wait for an answer before shouting, "Need any help canvassing the neighborhood to look for Mr. Johnson? He's probably in someone's backyard playing on their swing set."

"Any help from the community would be great, Frank," Officer Smith answers.

"How can I help?" I interject.

"You two should work together," he says, pointing to Frank. "Frank knows this neighborhood like the back of his hand, and the neighbors trust him. We have a lot of ground to cover before nightfall."

I roll my eyes, wishing I didn't have to work with the pain-in-the-ass, know-it-all Frank. However, the officer is correct; there's no time to waste. My body tingles with excitement at the thought of solving a case. I plop down in the passenger seat of the golf cart and tell Frank to drive by my house first so I can let Martha know what's going on.

"Oh no. Mr. Johnson's daughter must be so concerned," Martha worries.

"I will bring Mr. Johnson home safe and sound," I promise, wrapping my arms around her. "Don't wait on me for dinner."

She hands me a water bottle and a granola bar. My sweet Martha is always looking out for my best interest.

"Let's start on your street," Frank suggests. "You didn't see Mr. Johnson today because you were busy at the police station pestering the officers," he chuckles.

"I was taking care of important business," I tell him before heading to my backyard.

He follows me like a lost puppy. There's not a thing out of place. We walk a few houses down, looking in garage windows and calling for Mr. Johnson. Frank rings the bell when we get to Dave and

Ashley's house. Ashley opens the door a crack, sees me and opens the door wider.

"Hi, Walter. Are you here with my half of the winnings?" she whispers and smiles sweetly.

I beam and start to answer just as Frank yells, "We are looking for this man," He pushes his phone past me, through the door, right into Ashley's face. "He lives a street over and has Alzheimer's."

A gruff voice shouts from the other room, "What the hell is all that noise?"

Ashley warily glances behind her and says calmly, "Nothing, honey. No worries."

She turns her attention back to Frank and me, but before anyone can speak, Dave pushes Ashley aside and glares at us.

My hand forms a fist at my side. Dave's lucky there's a screen door between us. I remind myself to remain calm as I explain we are looking for a lost older gentleman. Frank holds out his phone to show Dave the photo of Mr. Johnson.

"He ain't here," Dave growls, slamming the door in our faces.

"That man is a real jerk," Franks shouts as we head down the sidewalk. "If I were younger and still on the force, I would kick his butt and throw him in jail!"

At least we can agree on one thing. I say a silent prayer for Ashley's safety.

We canvas the rest of the neighborhood. Frank shows every neighbor a picture of Mr. Johnson while I check garages and backyards. Mr. Johnson is not here. We end our search at the police station to submit our findings to the officer in charge. A younger officer is consoling Mr. Johnson's daughter. The lead detective decides to alert the media so they can get the word out.

Frank plants himself on a bench outside to watch for the media crew. I lean against the flagpole. No way am I leaving.

After the camera crew has their equipment set up, the Chief invites Frank and me to stand with him. I'm able to jockey to a good position right behind the Chief. Frank manages to sneak in beside me.

"Tomorrow Officer Smith, along with community officers Walter and Frank, will organize a city-wide search," the Chief speaks to the camera. "If you can, please join them at 9 o'clock at Creekside Park. With everyone's help, I know we can bring Mr. Johnson home to his loving family."

I stick my chest out a little more at the mention of my name and remind myself not to look too delighted. A vulnerable man is missing, after all. But I love nothing more than being part of a search and rescue. When I find Mr. Johnson, the reporters will interview me, and only then will I smile as the cameras show the world what a real hero looks like.

Following the press conference, Officer Smith discusses the plan with Frank and me. He gives us a box of walkie-talkies and maps of the area. I take the time to highlight the different search areas so the maps will be ready for volunteers in the morning. The police station buzzes with adrenaline as I work. Every time an officer reports updated news over the scanner, my ears perk up. I'm secretly hoping they don't find Mr. Johnson tonight. The worst thing that could happen now is someone ruining my chance to be a hero.

87

Martha

The leftovers in the refrigerator look less than appetizing, so I pour myself a bowl of cereal and plop down in front of the television. Old Mr. Johnson couldn't have picked a better day to get lost. Now I can watch the *Who's Your Daddy?* season finale without Walter bothering me.

Before the show starts, I send Bonnie a quick text to ask how she's feeling.

Lots better and just in time!

She texts, including an audio clip of the theme song to *Who's Your Daddy?*

I'm glad you're feeling better. Tonight is a critical night in American history—silly face emoji.

We continue to text as we watch, putting in our guesses as to who belongs to which daddy. During the show's first hour, three people pick incorrect daddies, and a beefy security guard escorts them out the back door—no two-week vacation for them. We watch as they frantically try to call an Uber to come and pick them up. One starts walking away aimlessly, clearly distraught that his free vacation is over. Four people pick correctly. They climb into a stretch limo and are whisked away to the airport for the trip of a lifetime. Now it's down to two contestants, a male and female, and two daddies. And wouldn't you know it, they both picked the same daddy. I'm on the edge of my seat when an ad for toothpaste pops on the screen. I text Bonnie.

The suspense is killing me!

Me too!

The show comes back on. After a short recap, the daddy both contestants chose walks up to the young man and hugs him. "I'm your daddy," he says through his tears.

The young woman standing next to them looks crushed and holds back tears. The daddy turns towards her and wraps his arms around her. "I'm your daddy too," he says.

Twins separated at birth! I never saw that coming. And if that wasn't enough, it turns out their birth mom is the makeup artist working with the show for the last two months. As the new family cries and hugs each other, I tear up and text Bonnie.

Didn't see that coming. Now I'm crying.

Me too! They tricked us!

The only two people who remain on the stage are one daddy and the host. The daddy turns to the host and says, "I'm your daddy." The studio audience erupts in applause. The host and his daddy hug and leave to join the other contestants for two weeks of partying. My phone buzzes with another text from Bonnie.

Wow! That was a whirlwind adventure!

So many twists and turns! What will we watch now?

Nothing as good as that I'm sure!

It's ten o'clock, and Walter is still not home. I flip to the news. The Police Chief is holding a news conference. Walter stands as proud as a peacock right behind the Chief. At ten-thirty, I climb the stairs to get ready for bed. When I crawl between the freshly washed sheets, I lay right in the middle. I love sleeping next to Walter, but having the bed to myself is heavenly.

88

Journal

Now you might be judging me, and to be completely honest, I was almost judging myself. But then I remembered how many times that man had shown up at my house, ruining my peace and quiet. Who is the real victim here? Not his lazy daughter—that's for sure.

Don't worry your pretty little head. If he doesn't show up by tomorrow, I will join the search and go and find him myself. I would bet some friendly family took him in and is trying to get him to tell them where he lives. Or maybe he's sleeping under the stars enjoying nature. I bet he's having the time of his life whatever he's doing. The fresh air will be good for him. If his dimwit daughter knew the gift I gave them both, she would be thanking me and baking me a pie or something.

89

Walter

I wake with a crick in my neck. That's what I get for sleeping in the spare room and putting Martha's sleep needs above my own. She was so peaceful, sprawled out in the middle of our bed last night, and I didn't want to disturb her.

I'm the first to arrive at the park, of course. Ten minutes later, Officer Smith pulls up next to me.

"Thanks for getting here so early, Walter," he shouts. "Mr. Johnson is still on the loose." He chuckles like a lost older man is funny.

I set up the walkie-talkies and maps, so everything is ready when the volunteers arrive. Frank shows up two minutes before nine o'clock. Nothing like almost being late.

"Ready to play detective?" Frank teases me, handing me a cup of crappy gas station coffee.

Officer Smith smirks, and my insides burn with anger.

"I'm ready to serve my community to bring a compromised citizen home to his loving family." I fake smile. "Thanks for the cup of coffee. You shouldn't have." I take one sip and then throw the cup in the trash can.

The volunteers start rolling in a little after nine. Most are Mr. Johnson's daughter's friends, and I recognize a few neighbors. Frank uses his loud voice to gather all the volunteers so Officer Smith can give directions. We hand out the maps and the walkie-talkies. Mr. Johnson's daughter passes out fliers with her dad's photo, her phone number, and information about a five hundred dollar reward, to post on every light pole.

Officer Smith releases the volunteers. The only areas not claimed are two sections on the outskirts of town. One is Highland Park, and the other is the outlet mall where I used to work. Officer Smith asks Frank and me if we can handle the last two spots.

"Sure, I can go find him," Frank screams. "I could always use an extra five hundred big ones. Want your old stomping ground?" he yells to me.

"Nah. I'll take the park," I tell him.

If Mr. Johnson were at the mall, the security guard who took my place undoubtedly would have already located him. After all, one of the most critical parts of mall security work is keeping current with the latest news. Any good security guard knows that.

90

Martha

The house is silent when I open my eyes. It's been years since I've slept this well. One look in the spare room explains my incredible night's sleep. The bed is a disaster. Walter's dirty clothes lay on the ground, surrounded by my beautiful decorative pillows and blankets. I shake my head—better tackle the laundry today. Walter left a note on the chalkboard that he's supervising the missing person case. I smile—another day with the house all to myself. I drink my coffee on the front porch in peace. I could get used to this.

91

Walter

The logical thing to do is to look in the neighborhood surrounding Highland Park. There are at least thirty homes. I knock on all the doors and show anyone who answers a picture of Mr. Johnson. No one has seen him. I tape fliers to every light pole just in case he shows up later.

After a walkie-talkie check-in with Officer Smith, I head to the park entrance. The park is large, with a wooded hiking area to the rear. A small building, next to a wooden play structure, houses restrooms. I'll start my search there. My eyes water from the stench in the men's room. Brown stagnant water sits in one of the urinals, and something resembling vomit is in the middle of the floor leading to the one stall. I shimmy around the green puddle and hit the door with my elbow, slamming it against the wall with a loud thud causing an echo to reverberate through the small room. Thank God Mr. Johnson is not here. Once I'm back outside, I take a deep breath of fresh air to clear the remnants of the nasty funk from my nasal cavity.

Next, I knock on the ladies' room door and shout, "Community officer. I'm looking for a lost citizen. Is anyone inside?"

No one answers.

I push the door open and yell, "Male community officer looking for a lost citizen," once more before entering.

The last thing I want to do is scare someone while they're taking care of business. At least the smell in here is not nearly as bad as the stench in the men's room. There is even a hint of lavender in the air. They must use fancy soap for the ladies.

Searching the playground equipment is next on my list. All of the slides and tunnels are empty—no Mr. Johnson. Before heading to the trail entrance, I check each tree just in case he fell asleep or passed out under one of them. No luck. I hope Frank is having the same luck as I am. He will never let it go if he finds old Mr. Johnson first.

The wooded section with the walking trail is the last area I need to search. A sign at the entrance shows the path is three miles. It also informs me that the hike is moderate level. I sigh, wishing I had taken the outlet mall instead. At least everything is flat and you can drive around and see most of it from your car. I wipe the sweat from my forehead and yell for Mr. Johnson. What are the chances he would be in the middle of these woods anyway? How could an eighty-year-old man with Alzheimer's hike a three-mile trail? I call one more time and decide my time would be better spent hanging up more fliers instead of walking in the woods. I tape a flier on the informational sign and two more near the entrance to the trails.

Back at my car, I crank the air and speak loud and clear into my walkie, "Walter at Highland Park. All clear. Over."

No response. The battery is dead, so I drive back to Creekside Park to check in and get a new one. When I pull into the parking lot, three local news channels have cameras pointed at Officer

Smith and Frank. My stomach plummets. I hurry over just in time to hear Officer Smith say, "Mr. Johnson has been found safely by one of our local citizen officers, Frank. You might remember Frank from his decades of service on the force and his years as head of the community outreach program."

"Where was he found?" one reporter asks, shoving his microphone in their direction.

Frank looks blankly at the reporter, not saying a word. Deaf as a stone.

Officer Smith jumps in, "Mr. Johnson was found at the outlet mall. He was sleeping on some boxes behind Aunt Annie's Pretzels."

"Do you know how Mr. Johnson got to the mall?" another reporter shouts.

"We do not suspect foul play. However, Mr. Johnson was unable to answer any questions at this time. He has been admitted to the hospital for evaluation and possible treatment of dehydration. As soon as we are able, we will question Mr. Johnson."

"Do you consider yourself a hero?" a pretty brunette reporter shouts to Frank.

Of course, he hears this question.

"I just did what any upstanding community member would do. I searched for a neighbor in need. I would not use the word hero. However, I won't argue with you if you do." He grins his big stupid smile.

Officer Smith says, "I would like to thank the media for your partnership in bringing Mr. Johnson home, and I would like to thank all the citizens who did their part in the search. We are truly blessed to live in a community that comes together and supports its most vulnerable citizens."

Officer Smith clears his throat, done with the press conference. Frank stands there looking at the cameras like an idiot. I bring my walkie-talkie over to a box on a picnic table and toss it in. The darn thing bounces against the others and ends up on the ground. I turn and walk as fast as I can to my car—not bothering to pick it up.

"Walter!" Frank shouts my name.

I pretend not to hear him. There is no way I am taking time out of my day to listen to him boast.

92

Journal

Are you happy now? Found safe and sound—not even twenty-four hours later. Only had a little dehydration. Nothing a glass of water couldn't fix. How hurt can you be if the cure is a little bit of water? He probably ate those pretzels right out of the trash. I'm sure he didn't even think of getting a drink from the fountain to go with all that salt.

While I was watching the press conference on the boob tube, Officer Smith said the whole community came together to find old Mr. Johnson. I did that. Brought everyone together with a common goal. A lovely feel-good story for the news too. Something happy for a change, all because of me.

I hope that lazy good-for-nothing daughter of his will keep track of her daddy now, or else Adult Protective Services may need to get involved and find him a safe place to live where he will be cared for properly.

93

Martha

The door slams shut in Walter's wake. His heavy footsteps stomp across the worn linoleum on the kitchen floor.

"Did you see the press conference?" he yells, even though I am sitting less than six feet from him at the kitchen table.

"The one about Mr. Johnson? What good news," I say in a cheery voice.

"Did you see Frank say he's a hero? Hero, my ass. I coordinated the search, and he had the easiest place to look. I took the park and dealt with disgusting bathrooms and a three-mile hike in the woods," he huffs as he plops down in the chair next to me.

"The important part is that Mr. Johnson is safe. Does it matter who found him?" I ask and gently lay my hand on his.

He yanks his hand away and stands so quickly that his chair falls to the floor, causing me to jump.

"There was a five hundred dollar reward! So I would say yes, it does!" he shouts, pacing. "Frank will rub it in my face that he found him and got the money. And the worst part is, he found him where I used to work. I will never live this down!"

"Everyone knows you were in charge of the search. No one would have found Mr. Johnson if it wasn't for you. How about a hot shower?" I suggest. "I will make you something to eat."

"No one will know I had anything to do with it! Frank and Officer Smith were the only people in the press conference. I can't believe I wasted my time for absolutely nothing."

He kicks off his shoes, not noticing the dirt flying in every direction. Next, he strips off his community officer shirt and throws it in the garbage can.

"I'm done giving my time to this community! I can't even keep my neighbor from being abused, let alone solve big cases!"

Maybe I should bring up that he found Peaches. But I think better of it; he's feeling way too sorry for himself. He slowly ascends the stairs. Two minutes later, when I hear the shower, I grab his shirt from the trash and add it to the next load of laundry. Maybe tomorrow, he will reconsider. I make him a turkey sandwich and leave it on the coffee table with a whole bag of his favorite chips.

94

Journal

I couldn't sleep, so I decided a stroll might be just what the doctor ordered. My therapist used to say, "Daily exercise is important for your mind and body." She must not have listened to her own words because she couldn't even do her job.

I heard footsteps behind me not more than a block into my walk. When I glanced over my shoulder, you won't believe who was following me like a lost puppy. The old geezer was back already, still wearing a hospital gown, for Pete sake. Once he saw my face, he started yelling that he wanted to go back to the park. I told him in my calmest voice to go home because it was time for bed. He just kept repeating he wanted to go back to the park.

The next thing I knew, his incompetent daughter was running down the road barefoot. She asked him why he was outside, and you won't believe what he said! He told her he wanted me to take him back to the park— no time like the present for a bit of back pedaling. I swore to her, hand to God, that I didn't take him to no park. He insisted I took him to the park to play but left him behind. Then she got right in my face and yelled at me. The nerve of some people. What happened to respecting your elders? She said if she found out I took him to the park, she would have me arrested. If she would watch her old man, then none of this would have happened in the first place.

So I told her that if either of them came near me or my house again, I would call the police and have them arrested for trespassing. Then I'd call Adult Protective Services and tell them about how she doesn't care for her daddy. She turned in a huff, grabbed his hand, and dragged him back to their house. And wouldn't you know it? The nitwit turned around and yelled, "See you at the park."

95

Martha

Today is my last self-defense class. I'm going to miss it. After a quick review of everything we have learned, Titus tells us to partner up for one final practice. The high school senior asked to be my partner. I am honored. The young woman has a good sense of humor and dry wit. Her assessments of the others in the class are spot-on and funny.

"Looks like you are enjoying class today," her grandma, Julie, comments.

"Sure am, Grams. Miss Martha is way better than any of my other partners," she says, mocking Julie when she turns back to her partner.

I turn and pretend to sneeze to cover my laughter. The impression of her grandma is dead-on. Titus invites us back to the circle of chairs where it all started.

"I would like to recognize everyone's hard work and determination with achievement awards," he tells us. "Trying something new at any age is hard. I hope you are proud of your work and will carry what you have learned with you."

The high school senior receives the *Best Granddaughter Award* for hanging out with her grandma on Saturdays. Julie gets the *Best Grandma Award* for doing her part to keep her granddaughter safe. Her granddaughter hugs her, and for a moment, I forget how much Julie annoyed me.

Titus hands out an award for each class member, calling my name last.

"Martha, I want to recognize you for going above and beyond. You possess a natural ability and continually persevere by putting in one hundred percent each week. Therefore I would like to give you the top award for *Best Overall Performance.*"

The class applauds while Titus presents my award.

He shakes my hand, looking me right in the eyes when he says, "I am proud of all you accomplished in this class."

I hug him and bite my tongue to keep from crying. I can't remember the last time anyone said they were proud of me.

96

Walter

I head straight to the bank after dropping Martha at her class. I feel sick that I was forced to move all of Martha's money into our joint account. I keep telling myself everything will be fine after I pay the bills and win back the money to replenish her account. She will never need to know, and God knows it's my turn to win big.

All of my senses come alive when I step into the casino. The air is electric—excitement courses through my body. I have already proven that the best course of action to win big money is sports betting. I divide my money between four different afternoon ball games. It's a sure thing I will win more than five hundred dollars, making up for the reward money that should have been mine. What a fiasco that turned out to be.

I place my bet slips in my wallet for safekeeping. The best place to watch the games would be from a bar stool, with an ice-cold beer, staring at the wall of TV screens in the bar. Unfortunately, I can't because I need to pick Martha up soon. I'll have to flip between the channels at home. Not ideal, but necessary.

When I pull into the community center parking lot, I don't see

Martha. I probably had time for one beer at the casino after all. Oh well—I might as well do something useful while I wait, so I count the rest of the cash in my wallet. To my pleasant surprise, I find some scratchers. I don't remember buying them, but I have been distracted lately. There's no time like the present. I start scratching before Martha makes her appearance. Three are defective, but the last one is a ten-dollar winner. It's the sign I needed that today is my day. I glance up to see Martha headed my way. I have just enough time to slip the winner into my wallet and throw the losers under my seat.

As soon as we get home, I grab the remote and search for the ball games. They start in thirty minutes. I go to the bathroom, pull out my slips and try to memorize my bets. I wish Martha wasn't such a stickler about gambling, because having them in front of me would be much easier.

97

Martha

Walter's terrible mood has carried over and intensified since yesterday. He didn't even ask how my last class went on the ride home. As soon as we stepped foot in the house, he grabbed the remote and started searching for something on TV. Every fifteen minutes, he races to the bathroom. Maybe stomach issues are causing his bad mood. Regardless, I'm not going to let him spoil my good mood. I post my certificate on the fridge, right at the top. Walter doesn't care about my achievement. However, I tell myself that the person I wanted to notice my improvements already has.

Walter is so engrossed in channel surfing he doesn't even notice the sandwich I set on the coffee table for him. I don't mind eating alone. Between his foul mood and the constant channel changing, he's driving me nuts. I'll go to the store and pick up a cake to celebrate my achievement. Maybe some sugar will help improve Walter's mood too.

"Need anything from the store?" I yell, already halfway out the door.

98

Walter

Martha yells something and slams the door, jolting me out of my daze. A sandwich sits on the coffee table. My stomach rumbles, and I remember I missed breakfast. I grab the sandwich and wolf it down. With Martha gone, I lay my bet slips on the coffee table and start tracking my winnings.

My head pounds as I switch from one game to the other. I come up short on three games, but I win by a landslide on the last one. I'll have to wait to cash in my winnings because it looks like Martha took the car. Where in the world did she go? I slide the winning bet slip into my wallet for safekeeping. The bag is almost full when I throw the losers in the trash can. Better to be safe than sorry, so I take the bag to the bin outside. Maybe Martha will notice how helpful I am.

99

Martha

Walter's mood is a bit better when I get home. Unfortunately, it doesn't last. The bathroom sink goes from a consistent drip to a constant stream of water. He has to cut off the water to the faucet. When I suggest going to the hardware store to buy a replacement or hire a plumber, he stomps out of the house without even replying. A minute later the car squeals out of the driveway. I roll my eyes and text Bonnie to see if she wants to pick me up for another hike.

100

Walter

I don't know what's gotten into Martha lately, but her mood has been terrible. I better get to the casino to cash out my winning bet so I'll have money for that annoying faucet.

The main parking lot is full, so it's the overflow lot for the win. I take a picture of my spot and then hike to the front doors. My first stop is the cashier to cash out my winning slip. With five hundred dollars in my hand, I decide a few bets on the slots is a good idea. I see a solid gold faucet in Martha's future. Maybe then she'll quit her nagging and leave me alone.

I sit down at my favorite machine, Gold Bar Rush. The rules are simple, place max bet, get three gold bars across the middle line, and win the jackpot. At the moment, the pot is worth $7,200. I slide all five crisp one hundred dollar bills into the machine. I can make a lot of home improvements with seven thousand dollars.

"Are you cheating on me?" a sweet voice asks, making me jump and causing me to spill my free soda on the floor.

When my eyes finally focus, I recognize the woman. It's Fran from the lotto counter. She wears shorts, a t-shirt with a cartoon dog, and a baseball cap—her hair pokes out every which way.

"I'm so sorry. I didn't mean to startle you," Fran says, holding my empty cup apologetically.

"Wow. I wasn't expecting to see you here," I stammer.

My cheeks burn with heat, and I try to recover. "But what a nice surprise. You are my lucky charm, after all."

"I wasn't much luck for your soda," she jokes, looking down where the remaining puddle seeps into the patterned carpet.

"Do you come here often?" she asks.

"Not that often. I won a bet on a couple of baseball games today and stopped by to cash in. Thought I would continue my lucky streak at my favorite slot machine. How about you?"

"My favorite hiking trail is nearby, and my friend lives close, so we meet here to grab a bite to eat now and then. The food is tasty, and they keep the prices low to draw people in so they can take all their money through these machines." She smiles that sweet smile of hers.

"I love to hike in the park while I patrol for criminal activity," I say, ignoring her comment about the slot machines. I've won plenty of money here.

"What kind of criminal activity?" she asks.

"Oh, you know, kids wreaking havoc, drug deals in the parking lot, or maybe even a murder," I say, trying to keep the excitement out of my voice. I don't want her to think I'm strange.

"That would be a good place for a murder. I'll keep that in mind if anyone does me wrong." She smiles, one eyebrow raised.

"Remind me never to go hiking with you," we both laugh at my joke.

"I suppose it wouldn't hurt to put a few bucks into one of these machines while I wait for my friend to show up," she says, sliding a five-dollar bill into the slot.

That won't get her far, but I'm glad she's sticking around to chat. This is nice. It's too bad Martha won't go to the casino with me.

Fran knows more about the neighborhood than I do. Whose marriage is on the rocks, and which teenager is knocked up. She asks if I was part of the search team to find Mr. Johnson.

"Sure was. I organized the investigation."

"You organized the investigation? What does that entail?" she asks, looking at me with awe.

"Well, the first day, I went door to door with the missing person fliers and looked in garages and backyards. The next day, I realized it was time to expand the search, so I divided the town into zones. I sent volunteers to search areas where someone in Mr. Johnson's condition might end up, all while keeping track of everyone's progress. I made sure no stone was left unturned and personally searched Highland Park. It was a big area, but I could handle it," I tell her, absentmindedly hitting the spin button on my machine.

"That's great, Walter. You know how to get things done," she says, reaching over to touch my arm. "Because of you, he was found quickly. I hope his daughter learned a lesson and will keep a better eye on him. The moms with toddlers are better at keeping track of their kids than she is at keeping track of her daddy. You don't even want to know how many times I've seen him put candy bars down his pants at the store," Fran sighs heavily. "I guess it's smart on his part. No way would we ask for it after it's been down there. Last week, he knocked three jars of spaghetti sauce off the shelf. A customer almost fell trying to maneuver the sauce river. The store manager told his daughter she needed to keep a better eye on him, or they wouldn't be allowed in the store anymore. His daughter was so offended she threatened to call the Better Business Bureau. She acted like it was our job to watch him so she could do her shopping."

"Who is your favorite customer?" I ask sheepishly.

"You, of course," she says with a smile.

My heart skips a beat. I'm glad Fran looks at her phone to distract from my burning cheeks, which I'm sure are bright red.

"My friend is on her way in," she tells me, pushing the button to print her ticket. "I'm up a hundred dollars!" she cheers. "Gambling is so much fun when you win!"

She hugs me and thanks me for keeping her company. I print out my ticket from the machine, and my heart sinks. I'm down to twenty-four dollars. Panic sweeps through my entire body as blood rushes to my head, making me feel dizzy. I was having such a pleasant talk with Fran that I wasn't paying any attention to my bets. All of my winnings are gone, and I still need a faucet. I trudge to the machine to cash out.

I drive to the hardware store on autopilot. What am I going to do? Martha will be in an even worse mood if I don't come home with a faucet. My feet feel like I'm wearing concrete boots as I make my way to the faucets. My only hope now is to find something in the clearance section.

"What's sup bro?" a chipper voice disturbs my thoughts.

I look over to see the kid standing too close to me.

"Not much. I need a faucet, and I only have twenty-four dollars. Do you have any good deals?" I ask hopefully.

"Man, bro, that isn't much money," he shakes his head, and it feels like all the blood drains from my body.

"You don't look too good, gramps. Are you feeling okay?" the kid asks with concern, or maybe it's pity.

"I'm okay. Just have had some bad luck these last couple of days."

"I hear ya. I had some bad luck myself. My gramps died last week."

He looks at me with glistening eyes, and I see him clearly for the first time. His childlike smirk, tousled hair, and sad eyes. I reach out to touch his arm.

"I am so sorry to hear that. I bet your gramps was really proud of you."

"I hope so," he says quietly, looking down at the floor.

"If I had a hard-working, caring grandson, who was maybe a bit of a chatterbox, I would be proud of him," I say honestly.

"Thank you. You remind me of my gramps. I'm sure you would have liked him. I sure did."

"I bet I would have. I like his grandson." I pat him on his back, and he beams.

The only faucet I can afford is junk. The back of the box might as well advertise, guaranteed to leak all over the floor, causing thousands of dollars in damage.

"Don't get that one bro. It will bust in a week. How about this one?" He picks up a faucet that would look great in my bathroom, but the sale tag says forty-five dollars.

"I can't afford it even with the sale." I shake my head.

"Sure you can. It has an open box discount," the kid says, opening the sealed box. "Looks like someone opened this one. Might be missing a part or the directions. Better mark it down."

I follow him to the small desk at the end of the aisle. He digs through the drawer, pulls out a fifty percent off sticker, and slaps it on the box.

"Won't you get in trouble for marking it down?" I question.

"Nah, they love me here." He grins his crooked smile.

I take the faucet from him and can't resist hugging him.

"I'm sorry about your gramps. Wish I could have met him."

"Thank you, sir," he says, hugging me back.

The kid follows me to the cashier to ensure she rings it up correctly. I am left with two dollars to my name.

"Hope your luck turns around," he calls over his shoulder as I leave.

101

Journal

Daily exercise in my neighborhood is out of the question. Not with that lunatic accusing me of driving him to the park. I was furious that I couldn't stroll in my neighborhood anymore. But my mama always said, "There ain't no reason you can't get glad in the britches you got mad in." I decided to mosey on up to the mountain hiking trails all by my lonesome so I wouldn't be bothered.

I parked my car in the almost deserted parking lot. Even though it was hotter than the devil's armpit, it was a perfect day to hike the cliff trail. My mood improved as I listened to the birds chirping their merry songs, and I laughed right out loud when a chipmunk ran over my shoes.

The easy trail is my favorite because it's the perfect length and loops back around to the parking lot. An hour later, I was back where I started, as happy as a hound dog sitting on the front porch with a bone. I leaned against the trail entrance sign to retrieve a small pebble rattling around in my shoe. That's when I saw him. The good-for-nothing was sitting in his car not more than fifty feet from where I stood. I would recognize Dave's greasy black hair anywhere. He looked as relaxed as a pig in a mud bath. A smile grew across his face, and his eyes popped open. He looked right at me, and I swear on my daddy's grave, he winked at me. The next thing I knew, a woman's head popped up from his crotch. She wiped her mouth, jumped out of the passenger door, and waltzed over to his door. He handed her cash, and she scurried to a car waiting at the entrance. I nearly didn't believe what my eyes were seeing. That no good, dirty, rotten weasel.

He reached for the sandwich sitting on his dash and took a bite like nothing had happened. He just ate his sandwich and then drove down the mountain road. I was so dumbfounded it was like my feet were in quicksand, and I couldn't move. What he's doing to his wife and kid is bad enough, and now this! Right in broad daylight. The lowlife has no shame, and he's wasting his family's money to boot.

Don't you worry. I'm fixing to find a way to wipe that wicked grin from his smug face and serve up some justice for his family.

102

Martha

Today is a beautiful day for painting class. I turn on Walter's police scanner before I leave the house to walk to the park. Maybe there will be a crime he can focus on.

Bonnie waves me over with a massive smile on her face. I am reminded of how thankful I am to have a good friend. We learn a new technique and begin creating our paintings while we catch up. During a rare moment of silence, I ask Bonnie how her daughter is doing.

"Not well." Bonnie shakes her head. "We only see her when Dave isn't home, and since he's not working right now, he's home a lot. I can only spend time with my grandson when he goes to the mountains to "exercise." To be honest with you, I think he's dealing drugs or worse up there. Someone threw a rock through their front window. It said, 'For the wages of sin is death.' Can you believe that? I thought we lived in a safe community."

"I am so sorry. This all seems so stressful." I try to think of something better to say to ease her pain, but my mind is blank.

"Ashley invited us over as soon as he left yesterday. She was so nervous we only stayed for fifteen minutes. After we left, I tried to think of a way that the situation could work out with her and Charlie unharmed. The only thing I know is, the longer she stays with him, the worse it gets."

"Do you think she would go to therapy? It might help her get the strength to leave that good-for-nothing ass..." I stop talking before my anger takes over.

"We have offered to pay for counseling for her and Charlie. She won't go. She says Dave doesn't want her gossiping about all their problems to a stranger. Trevor is so worried he called Deaven at the pawn shop to ask if he has any unregistered guns. Thank God Deaven told him no. It was a good choice. I certainly don't think Trevor would thrive in prison for murder."

"Woah. You both must be so worried about what might happen."

"Honestly, I'm worried about what is happening. Dave has turned my beautiful daughter into a shell of the person she used to be."

"I wish there was something I could do," I tell her honestly.

"I'll let you know when I need help hiding the body. Or an alibi." She laughs.

I'm hoping she is just trying to lighten the mood.

103

Walter

Martha's favorite coffee cup is sitting in the sink. She must have already left for her painting class. Static comes over my police scanner. I don't remember leaving it on, but I listen while I drink my coffee. Nothing exciting is happening. A few traffic stops at the usual speed trap and a small kitchen fire that is rapidly extinguished. I decide to log into the bank account. Depression hits when I see the balance. There's not enough left to pay the bills.

I walk through the house, searching for anything I can sell. Starting in the basement, I search through boxes, my dad's old tools are the only things I find with potential. It's a start. On the main floor, I find the boys' old skis in the back of a closet. They might bring a few bucks. Upstairs in our bedroom, I search Martha's jewelry box. Most of her pieces are costume jewelry and are not worth anything. The ring she bought at the estate sale sits in its own compartment. I hold it up to the window and the morning light catches the stone. It is stunning. She hasn't worn it, and the pawnshop guy said it's worth a pretty penny. Although I would hate for her to notice it's gone. I'll keep it in mind just in case, but hopefully, the tools and skis will bring in enough for me to pay the bills.

As I drive to the pawn shop, I reminisce about the good times with my dad. It will be hard to let his tools go. They are the last part of my dad I have besides the memories. When I win big, I vow to get them back.

The door chimes, signaling my entrance to the empty shop. A young man covered in tattoos enters from the back.

"Good morning sir. How may I help you today?" he asks, looking me right in the eyes.

I love the respect he offers.

"I have some tools and skis I would like to sell," I inform him.

I lean the skis against the counter and set the box of tools down with a thud. He removes the tools, one at a time, inspecting each with care. Next, he takes a closer look at the skis and the bindings. He enters some information into his laptop.

"I can give you one fifty for all of it," he says, looking up from his screen.

"Sure. Sounds good," I agree.

While I fill out the paperwork, I ask about the buyback program. For a ten percent markup, I can get the tools back. That's my plan.

Next, I drive to the bank to deposit one hundred dollars into the account, praying it's enough to cover the bills. The remaining fifty is for groceries. I don't want Martha using the debit card. When I slide the money into my wallet, I see my winning scratcher. Better stop by the store to grab a few more winners.

Fran isn't working today. Instead, Ashley stands behind the service counter.

"Good morning," she greets me cheerfully.

The makeup on her face is thick.

"What happened? It looks like you have a nasty bruise," I inquire kindly.

"I am such a klutz. I tripped over a toy and smacked my face into the wall. I need to be more careful," she tells me nervously.

I hand her my winning ticket and ask for two five-dollar scratchers.

"If you need my help, I can be there in less than a minute," I say in a low, calm voice when she returns with my tickets. "I can be the one to press charges if you aren't able to." I grab a lotto form, write my number on it, and hand it to her. "Call me anytime, day or night. Your life doesn't have to be like this."

"I'm okay. I will call if we need some sugar or something, and you can come right down."

I get in the car, too wound up to scratch the tickets, so I shove them in my wallet. I make a pit stop at the senior center and take an entire box of donuts. When I get home, I sit on the front porch eating donut after donut, trying to formulate a plan to help her. I come up with nothing but indigestion.

104

Martha

When I return home, Walter is in a worse mood than before. He's pacing between the kitchen and the living room. His police scanner is so loud I can hear it upstairs. I know he's upset, but when I ask him, he snarls at me and says don't worry about it. I feel like I'm sitting next to a sleeping bear. At any moment, he is going to wake up and attack.

"Are you going to work a community patrol shift this week?" I ask, hopeful it will give him something to do.

"Why would I bother? I can't even keep my own neighbor safe."

"Which neighbor is unsafe?" I ask, but I'm positive he knows something about Dave abusing Ashley and sweet little Charlie.

"I told you it's nothing for you to worry about," he mutters.

The pacing continues—kitchen, living room, porch, down the street, and then all over again. I pray for a crime to come across the scanner—anything to get Walter out of this loop. But there are only traffic stops, for Pete's sake.

105

Journal

I went to work right when I got home from my walk. Busier than a moth in a mitten, as my mama would have said. I was hell-bent on removing that piece of crap from the face of the earth.

I found the spare keys to the old car I sold ages ago and scrubbed them until they were as shiny as a freshly minted nickel. Don't you worry, I wore gloves. I drove back to the park with the key ring safely in my pocket. I walked the trail next to the cliff and climbed over the wooden fence by the warning sign. Like a little fence or sign will prevent someone from a terrible fall.

I threw the keys over the edge and grabbed a tree branch to watch them fall. I thanked the Lord they landed perfectly on the ledge after a little bounce. Just a sign from up above that I'm doing the right thing.

106

Martha

I wake to the sound of the police scanner blaring. Speed trap got another one. Too bad he has a warrant. I'm guessing we are both going to have a bad day.

Walter is already in the kitchen, more upset than yesterday. I ask how he's doing, but he grunts and walks away. It's not even nine a.m. yet, and my head is pounding. I don't bother telling Walter before going to lay in bed with a cold cloth on my face.

107

Walter

I can't stop pacing. I don't know what to say to make Dave stop hurting Ashley. The only thing I can do is keep an eye on that good-for-nothing. I vigilantly monitor their house. He will not harm her today without me knowing and alerting the authorities.

On one of my house patrol checks, the mailman hands me my mail. Another past-due notice is right on top of the pile. I rip it open to see the cable company is threatening to turn off our cable in three days if we don't pay in full. After years of being a loyal customer, this is how they treat me. The next time Martha is gone, I'll call and give them a piece of my mind. They should be ashamed of themselves for taking advantage of retired people.

I hide the bill in the desk drawer and wander to the garage to look for something else to sell. I can't find a thing. Not even scrap metal. The newspaper is on the porch waiting for me. I scour the pages for crimes to solve with a possible reward—nothing, not even a lost cat. I move on to the classifieds but quickly give up. There's no point. How would I explain to Martha that I want to be a janitor?

I continue pacing between our house and Ashley's.

108

Journal

Watching Dave's car became my full-time job. That son of a beehive wasn't budging. A couple of days later, I was out watering my flowers, enjoying the grass between my toes, and wouldn't you know it, that snake's car wasn't in the driveway. I ran into the house, slipped on the first pair of shoes I could find, and grabbed the car keys. On my way out of the neighborhood, I said a little prayer to our Heavenly Father that I hadn't missed my chance.

I'm not going to lie; I risked my life speeding up the mountain road. When I rounded the corner at the top, I almost ran into that no-good pimp's car. Dave's car was sitting in the corner under a giant oak. Jackpot! I backed into a spot near the trail entrance.

I barely made a peep getting out of my car, but something wasn't right when my feet hit the ground. I looked down and saw I wasn't wearing my own shoes, for Pete's sake. I had to tie them up real tight. It would have to do for now. I wasn't planning to go on a hike anyway. I shuffled to the spot where I had tossed the key ring—only stumbled once in the Bozo shoes. When I peered over the cliff ledge, there they sat, ready to do the Lord's work.

I went back to the car to keep an eye on things. I stood behind a giant oak and watched as the hussy finished her work. I wished I could teach her a lesson too, but that would have to wait for a different day. Once she left, Dave started chewing on his sandwich. Being a dirty bastard must make him hungry. He started his car, and I got worried he would take off, but he just rolled the windows up and sat there. Must have needed some air conditioning. I snuck up to his car as quietly as I could. He jumped when I tapped on his window, making me smile inside. He rolled his window down. The loser hadn't even bothered to zip his pants up. Lord have mercy. I jerked my eyes away real quick. I didn't need to be seeing any baby-making business today.

I swallowed the bile rising in my throat and talked to him real sweet. Told him how happy I was to see him and how my car keys slipped from my hand and fell down a small cliff. I told him I was in real trouble between forgetting my phone at home (you don't think I'm stupid enough to bring my phone to a crime scene, do you?) and the heat. I asked if he would be so kind as to help me. He lifted his nasty ass off the seat and zipped his pants, all the while smiling at me. My throat burned, and I would have liked nothing more than to spit on him. He told me this better be quick because he had to get home to babysit his kid. I promised I would put a good word in with Ashley about how helpful he was. He smiled like a shit-eating possum.

At the warning sign for the cliff edge, I saw a glimpse of the sissy he was. He didn't want to climb over the fence, telling me it was dangerous. Like he's afraid of a little danger. Numskull has never paid attention to a warning in his life. After I reassured him, he finally stepped over the fence. I let him go ahead, walking real slow behind him. He looked back once with a cautious grin. I just smiled at him real sweet.

He whined about not being able to see the keys. As my daddy liked to say, he was nervous as a long-tailed cat in a room full of rocking chairs. Took all I had not to laugh right out loud in his face. I encouraged him to go a little further so he could see the keys plain as day. I told him I had seen them with my own two eyes earlier, but my feeble bones couldn't make the climb down. He grunted and said he was only helping me because I reminded him of his dead mama. Well, bless his pea-pickin' little heart.

He shuffled his feet, getting closer to the end of the giant boulders, bent over, and looked over the cliff. Right at that very moment, the good Lord peered down from heaven and gave me the strength I needed to take care of this problem once and for all.

I grabbed hold of a nearby tree branch, raised my leg, and kicked him square in the ass as hard as I could. He lurched forward and stumbled. His arms flailed like one of those dancing wind guys down at the used car lot. With nothing to grab onto, he tumbled off the edge. I swear I heard his head bounce off the side of the rocks. God answered my prayers. He screamed like a little girl, and I was thankful the place was deserted. I heard the thump when he landed. I held as still as possible to listen for the aftermath, but the only thing that greeted my ears were the cicadas.

When it was all said and done, I looked down and saw my bare foot. I burst out laughing. The shoe I was wearing must have flown off when I kicked him. I carefully inched to the ledge on my hands and knees and peered over. Blood oozed from his head like a jelly donut that had been stomped on. Made my stomach rumble. I was thankful I didn't see a shoe. It wouldn't have mattered much anyway since it didn't belong to me, but it's always better not to leave evidence. Any dummy knows that.

On the drive home, I pulled into a little donut shop and ordered my favorite donut. You know, the one with pink icing and sprinkles. I sat in the car with the air conditioner blasting, savoring every last bite.

As soon as I got home, I buried the shoe in the bottom of the kitchen trash bag, topped it off with my fur baby's putrid litter, and took the bag to the garbage can. The only misfortune was that they had just picked up the trash yesterday, but I didn't care. No one would be looking through my trash, especially with the cat crap on the top.

I ended my marvelous day with my feet up, enjoying a Lifetime movie about a woman who shoots up her cheating husband while he screws the other woman. The wife gets away with it, of course. The world hates a man that is a piece of shit.

109

Martha

I wake up to constant pinging. My phone is blowing up with texts from Bonnie. Her piece of shit son-in-law didn't come home last night.

Dave has been gone all night. No word.

Ping

If it was up to me he could stay gone forever

Ping

Ashley and Charlie are upset so I guess we should look for him.

Ping

If Walter could have his friends on the force be on the lookout for his piece of shit car that would be great.

Ping

No rush, if you know what I mean.

Three smiley emojis follow the last text. I text back a thumbs up, a heart, and a winky face, so she knows I'm on it.

Walter is drinking his coffee at the kitchen table and perusing the paper. I tell him the news that Dave has gone missin', and his eyes brighten. He jumps up, almost spilling his coffee, and says he needs to start searching. He's out the door before I can respond.

The house is quiet. I drink my coffee in peace without Walter pestering me with his ever increasing lousy mood. After I tidy up, I decide it's time to relax and watch the boob tube. Three episodes of *My Neighbor's A Murderer* later, I grab a snack and flip to the news at noon. I do a double-take. I don't believe my eyes.

110

Walter

I know the perfect place to start my search. A quick stop at the senior center to grab a few donuts for the road will give me the energy I need. If the donut selection indicates how this day will turn out, I would say it's looking lucky. They have one of my favorites from childhood. Cake donuts with cherry frosting and sprinkles. I grab three.

I finish the donuts before I reach the winding road to my favorite hiking trails. Rounding the corner to the parking lot, I immediately spot Dave's old Toyota. Like a sore thumb, it sticks out in the otherwise vacant lot. I park two spots away from it and cautiously walk over. The car is empty except for a lunch bag and a baggie on the passenger seat.

I'll look around for a few minutes before I call the police. There's no way I'm giving up a chance again to be the hero. When opportunity knocks, you better listen. I don't even reach the entrance to the trail when I see the vultures circling above. There must be dozens of them. If I know one thing about vultures, they don't bother with anything alive. My breathing quickens with my pounding heart.

Carefully I climb over the fence next to the cliff warning sign. I shuffle to the edge, grab a tree branch for support, and peer over the ledge. Two vultures peck at my neighbor's face. His greasy jet-black hair is a dead giveaway. It's Dave.

My knees give way as I collapse to the ground near the edge. My breakfast lurches out of my mouth, cascading down the rocks, leaving a trail of sprinkles. I wipe my mouth with the back of my arm and slowly crawl backward, away from the ledge.

When I am safe, I lean against a tree to regain my composure. It feels like time stands still while I wait for my heart to return to a more regular rhythm. I fumble to retrieve my phone from my pocket. No signal. Standing on shaky legs, I slowly walk back towards the path, hoping to find a signal. I'm almost back to the parking lot when I finally get through to the 911 operator. I collapse on a bench and describe the horror I witnessed to the calm voice on the other end of the line. She assures me that help is on the way. I close my eyes and rub my forehead. The repulsive image reappears in my mind, and I turn to vomit again.

111

Martha

Walter is staring at me from the television screen. He looks like he's seen a ghost.

"I was searching for my neighbor. His mother-in-law is friends with my wife. The family was concerned because he didn't come home last night," he says in a shaky voice.

"Why did you search this park?" the reporter asks.

"Due to the experience I gained from being a security guard, I know this park is known for criminal activity. I drove up here so I could cross it off my list. I was surprised to see his car."

"After you spotted the car, what did you do?"

"I called the police to let them know. While I waited, I hiked up the trail calling for Dave. There was no answer. I spotted my neighbor's body when I searched the cliff edge."

"How are you doing after finding your friend dead?" A reporter yells from the back of the group.

"Honestly, Dave was not my friend. He was not a very good person. I had significant evidence that he abused his wife and child, and I shared that evidence with the police. I only wanted him charged with abuse, not found dead, mind you."

Walter looks down at his shaking hands. I haven't seen him this upset since his mom passed away.

"Thank you for taking the time to speak to us." The reporter quickly turns to question an officer who states they have no comment at this time because it is an open investigation. They will hold a press conference as soon as they can.

I call Bonnie.

"Did you hear the news?" I ask, hoping she did. I don't want to be the person to tell her.

"Ashley just called. We are on our way over to her house. I wanted him out of our lives, but I never thought it would happen this way," her voice catches.

"Is there anything I can do to help?"

"There is nothing anyone can do now."

I hang up, feeling bad for my friend and her family. I check the cupboards and fridge for ingredients for my famous mac and cheese and oatmeal raisin cookies.

112

Walter

I sit on the bench near the entrance to the trail, shivering despite the heat, rehashing the questions the officer asked me. I answered all her questions in detail. She asked what I was doing yesterday. A usual question, I presume, if you find a dead body. The police want to ensure you didn't find the body quickly because you put it there. She asked why I chose this park to hike today. I explained how it's a perfect spot to cover up a murder. Oh geez, maybe that was a mistake. She wrote every word I said in her notebook.

A different officer measured my foot and took pictures of the bottom of my shoes. I asked why they were so concerned with my shoes since I admitted to being at the crime scene. Hell, I walked them to the crime scene. He said it was so they would know which footprints didn't belong to me.

My stomach rolls inside me, but nothing is left, and I dry heave. I'm in no shape to drive, so I sit and sip the water one of the officers handed me earlier. I watch as the search and rescue team hauls their equipment down the trail. Every so often, a police officer walks by holding evidence bags. One has a gray tennis shoe in it, but I can't make out what's in the others.

An EMT comes to talk with me. She has a kind voice. After she wraps a crinkly, silver blanket around my shoulders, she asks me silly questions like what year is it? And who is the president? I confess that I can't get the image of my neighbor out of my head. She says she understands, but I doubt it. Has she ever seen a man getting his face pecked off by vultures? She asks if I want to go to the hospital. I decline, telling her I'm just waiting for them to bring his body up. Maybe knowing he's not down there anymore will give me a little peace. I have no idea how long I've been sitting there when the search team walks by with a stretcher. Dave's body lies lifeless in a black body bag. I want to go home to Martha. I trudge to my car and drive home on autopilot.

Relief washes over me when I pull into my driveway. Ashley rushes from her yard as soon as I get out of the car. She wraps me in a hug.

"Thank you for finding him," she says through her tears. "Did he look peaceful?"

"He did," I lie.

"They are going to do an autopsy. I can't see him until they are done. I don't think I will believe he's gone until I see him," Ashley says, staring at me through her red, puffy eyes.

"He'll look different than you remember. Death changes a person," I tell her, clasping her small hands in mine. "I think you should have your dad identify him."

I don't want the image of his pecked-out eyeballs in my head, and I'm sure as shit she won't want it in hers. Ashley hugs me, turns, and walks back up the street. I grab the mail and head to the house. The only thing I want to do is lay down. I quickly scan the envelopes and see a past-due bill from the gas company. This is the last thing I need right now. I stuff the envelope in a drawer in the desk. I'll deal with it tomorrow.

Martha has cookies on the counter and mac and cheese in the crock pot, but I can't bring myself to eat anything. I go lay down in bed and stare at the ceiling.

113

Martha

I find Walter lying on the bed, staring at the ceiling. He looks terrible. I sit near him and rub his arm.

"What happened?" I ask gently.

"You don't want to know," he mumbles.

His body shudders.

"I'll let you rest." I kiss his cheek and cover him with a blanket.

He rolls over to stare at the wall. I don't want to leave him alone in his state, so I put together my funeral attire. My black dress and shoes, with the one-inch heel, still fit. I quietly dig through my jewelry box to find my treasure. Slipping the ring on my finger makes me smile at the memory of the special day I shared with Bonnie. I admire my wardrobe choice in the full-length mirror, excited to show off my good taste. I sit the ring on the top of the dresser alongside a classy necklace that will complete my outfit.

114

Journal

When I see that poor girl on TV crying about her dead piece of shit husband, I am reminded of what my therapist said in that annoying voice of hers. "Sometimes you must sit with your feelings for a while to understand the true emotion. At times you might feel angry, but maybe you're feeling hurt. Or sometimes, excitement comes across as anxiety."

That girl thinks she's sad, but I know she's relieved and happy underneath. I will start a neighborhood fund to help with the funeral expenses. If it were up to me, I'd put him in a pine box, douse him in gasoline, and light a match. But I suppose, for the boy's sake, we should throw that good-for-nothing a proper funeral. Maybe I will organize a candlelight vigil at the hiking trails. It will be great to revisit that special place where the Lord handed down his judgment.

115

Walter

Every time I close my eyes, I see the birds pecking Dave's eyeballs out of his smashed head. I must have finally fallen asleep because the horror changes from the birds pecking Dave's eyes to mine. I wake up in a cold sweat and feel my face. My eyes are still where they should be.

I go to the bathroom and splash some water on my face. Better get dressed and start the day. I need to check on the banking before Martha wakes up. Something shiny catches my eye when I retrieve a clean t-shirt from the dresser. It's Martha's ring. I slip it into my pocket. The time has come to cash it in and get us caught up on the bills.

Sitting at the kitchen table with a steaming cup of coffee, I open the computer and log into the bank account. My stomach sinks. Three overdraft charges totaling ninety-nine dollars. The cable, gas, and electric bill have all bounced. Doing some quick math in my head, I realize we are short five hundred dollars. I'll wait for the mail before going to the pawn shop. The last thing I need is for Martha to see an overdue bill.

Martha comes down the stairs and seems giddy. She is glowing.

"I had the best idea last night!" she exclaims, pouring herself a cup of coffee.

"You should call Crime Stoppers," she says, sitting in a chair beside me. "I did a little research last night, and found out they pay up to twenty-five hundred dollars for tips on a homicide. You already practically solved the case. They should pay you something. We could use the money to take a vacation. Somewhere tropical." She hands me her phone with the Crime Stoppers number on the screen.

"That is a good idea. I did find Dave, which should be worth something."

I take her phone and head outside to call. Martha doesn't need to hear the grisly details.

116

Martha

Walter is still pale and in a daze. I'm not sure how long the symptoms of shock last. It might be a good idea to call the doctor to see if there is anything I should look out for. The clock on the microwave informs me the office won't be open for another hour. In the meantime, I might as well make myself useful, so I make the bed and pick up Walter's dirty clothes. His dresser drawer is still open, with several shirts hanging over the side. I shake my head at the realization that he will never change. Once a slob, always a slob.

After I shove his shirts back in the drawer, I glance at my funeral attire on the top of the dresser. Where's my ring? I am confident I put it right on top of my clothes after I tried it on last night. Maybe the cat knocked it off. Crawling on my hands and knees, I look under the dresser and the bed. I dig through the drawers and check my jewelry box, just in case. My ring is not there. It has to be here somewhere. I'll ask Walter if he's seen it when he done with his call. He probably put it somewhere for safekeeping. The bedside clock shows it's a little after nine. Better call the doctor's office before I forget. If we learned anything from yesterday, it's that life is precious.

I search the desk for my address book, but can't find it. I'm losing my mind. First, the ring, and now the address book. It has to be here. I remove all the papers, going through them piece by piece. Two envelopes have bright red past-due notices stamped on the front. I tear one open. The water bill. The second is last month's electric bill. My hands tremble as I frantically search the rest of the desk. I discover two more unopened past-due bills. What the hell happened to our money? My blood boils.

I open the computer to search the emails for clues. There is nothing in the main folder. However, when I open the little trash basket icon, I discover a barrage of emails from the bank. I open the statement from my personal account to see the measly balance of twenty-two dollars. My legs feel like jelly as I sink to the floor.

Walter has taken all of my money. That son of a bitch is gambling again. I'm an idiot for believing he could change. Once a liar, always a liar. My daddy always said that lies are like cockroaches. Once you find one, there are twenty more hiding under the fridge. I grab Walter's phone off the counter and scroll through his camera roll. Picture after picture of parking spaces at the casino. That piece of shit lost all our money. We can't even pay our bills, and my money is gone too. My body shakes with rage. Why did I trust him? People never change.

Walter walks into the family room. Before I can unleash my fury and give him a piece of my mind, I see something in his hand that makes me forget all about what I was going to say.

117

Walter

I call Crime Stoppers from the garden shed. When I inform the lady on the other end that I solved a missing person case yesterday, she explains that a case like that isn't a Crime Stoppers case. They are looking for tips from cold cases, homicides, or evidence that can lead to an arrest in wrongdoing. Missing person cases are apparently a dime a dozen.

"So you're telling me that if I would have found him a month after he went missing, then I could get a reward, but not the day after he went missing. What difference does it make? I still found him," I plead my case.

"I'm sorry, sir. If the authorities discover foul play and you solve the crime, there might be a reward," she says in her smug voice.

"This is bullshit," I scream, slamming the phone down on a rusty shelf.

I kick the stack of old plastic flower pots next to the door. A rainbow of weathered plastic and dirt flies in all directions. I huff, mumbling obscenities, and start picking up the pieces. When I tip the largest pot upright, I see something at the bottom. I reach in and poke the object. No movement. At least if it's an animal, it's dead. On closer inspection, it looks like fabric. I grab it and pull it out, dried soil flying everywhere. I recognize the sweatshirt. It used to be my oldest son's favorite when he was a teenager. What in the world is it doing out here? My super sniffer detects lighter fluid and dirt, but after Martha washes it, I'm sure it will be good as new. I'll wrap it up and give it to him for Christmas. Lord knows we can't afford real gifts this year.

On my way back to the house, I hear the familiar sound of the mail truck coming down the street. I take the long way around the house and head to the mailbox. He waves after shoving a stack of letters into our box. Perfect timing. I have made it my mission to get to the mailbox before Martha.

I scan the letters as I walk up the drive. A past-due phone bill is in the pile. I'll save a step and put it in the trash bin outside. I strain to grab the single bag at the bottom. The scent of soiled kitty litter fills my nostrils. I loosen the knot on the top, ignoring the smell, and push the bill to the bottom of the bag. Martha would be livid if she knew the state of our finances. As I bring my hand back up, it rubs against what feels like fabric. Which of my favorite t-shirts is Martha throwing out this time? I grab hold of the item and pull it out. It's my gray tennis shoe. I turn it over in my hands. I would bet my last dollar that this is the same shoe I saw in the evidence bag yesterday.

I walk into the house, clenching my son's old sweatshirt and the dirty shoe. A trail of cat litter follows me. Martha looks up from the computer with a look I've never seen in her eyes before.

She speaks to me through tight lips, hissing, "What the hell happened to my mon..."

Her words halt in her throat when she notices the items in my hands.

"I should call the police right now," I say, searching her face for the sweet, timid woman I thought I knew.

Her lips curl, and she sneers, "Maybe you should, but I don't think you will. Aren't you holding YOUR shoe? The perfect match to the one found at the scene of Dave's untimely death yesterday. Didn't you tell that reporter about what an abusive asshole Dave was? I do declare you willingly shared your motive on the television. If I were a betting person like you, I would wager that the police are curious as to how you knew where Dave's body was. I reckon they might be discussing your motive and means for killing poor Dave right this very minute. Like they always say on my crime shows, the killer often goes back to see HIS handiwork. Plus, from the look of our finances, you are far from innocent. My therapist always said when you point the finger at someone else, three fingers point right back at you. If you know what's good for you, you best put that shoe right back where you found it. You also might want to say a prayer that I don't turn YOU in. I wonder who they would believe if the police saw that shoe you're holding, with your fingerprints all over it. A sweet neighborhood grandma with tiny feet, or a bitter wannabe police officer with gigantic feet. It might be fun to find out. Don't you think? Now, take care of that nasty shoe and wash your hands. You disgust me."

I stare at her, unable to move. I have no words. I can't believe this is the same person I have been married to for over forty years. It feels like an eternity passes before I'm able to speak, "How could you?"

Martha smiles sweetly and says in a voice I no longer recognize, "I think the better question is, why couldn't you? You're the one who acts like it's your job to keep our community safe. But two houses down Ashley and Charlie are being abused and you did nothing except drive around in your golf cart like an idiot." She glares at me with her arms crossed. "I, like always, had to clean up everyone's mess. I only wish I could tell Bonnie because I know she would be so grateful I took care of the Dave problem."

Martha walks towards the stairs before continuing, "I made you one of your disgusting canned tuna sandwiches for lunch, and your suit is pressed and ready for the memorial service. You might want to practice your sympathetic face in the mirror just in case there are more reporters at the service to whom you want to confess your hatred of the deceased." She slowly walks up the stairs as I stand in shock, unable to move.

"And Walter, dear, quit gambling away my money, give me my ring, and get a job to pay me back, or I reckon you and I might find ourselves on a little hike." She laughs as she climbs the rest of the steps.

Thank You

Thank you for making our dream a reality by taking the time to read our book. We are honored that you chose to spend time with Martha, Walter, Bonnie, and Fran. We hope you love them.

Thank you to Mikey Ouding. You inspired this story with your quest to discover a dead body. You are the best of what Walter wishes he would be.

Thank you to Lori Branigan for reading this book at least four times. Your enthusiasm kept us going when we had a lot of work to do. I feel like you have been a positive person in my life for forever.

Thank you to Lisa Smith for reading this book several times and finding all the errors we missed. We could not have done it without you. Thank you for being my friend for 30 years and for all the support you have shown me and my family.

Thank you to J.L. Hyde. Your writing journey has inspired us. If you loved this book you will adore J.L. Hyde's work. Check out Delta County, Summer of '99, and Midnight in Delta County. I still can't believe that you read our book and gave us a review for the cover. Thank you for your support.

Thank you to our prereaders. Your honest feedback changed our book for the better in so many ways. Thanks to Tom Branigan, Shannon Brow, Shari Piccard, Beth Green, Yvonne Elliott, Ed Walker, Jeff Tillmann, Kathleen Knott, and Mary Brickner. Thank you for your honest reviews, encouragement, and support.

Thank you to our partners, Jeff and Ed. Your support and financial backing made this project possible and your encouragement got us through the rough patches.

If you loved Donuts and Deceit:

The single best thing you can do for an independent writer is to tell someone. Leave a review, make a social media post, or tell a friend. It may be a simple gesture to you, but to us it's everything.

Thank you for helping support our dream.

You, our reader, mean everything to us.
We would love to hear from you.

Visit us online at butterybraniganbooks.com
Email us at butterybraniganbooks@gmail.com
Visit us on social platforms: Buttery Branigan Books on
Facebook, TikTok, and Instagram.

We can't wait to hear from you!

Made in the USA
Las Vegas, NV
29 September 2023

78294302R10174